SAY CHEESE AND DIE—AGAIN!

Look for more Goosebumps books
by R.L. Stine:
(see back of book for a complete listing)

Goosebumps®

SAY CHEESE AND DIE—AGAIN!

R.L. STINE

AN
APPLE
PAPERBACK

SCHOLASTIC INC.
New York Toronto London Auckland Sydney

A PARACHUTE PRESS BOOK

ISBN 0-590-56881-7

12 11 10 9 8 7 6 5 4 3 2   6 7 8 9/9 0 1/0

Printed in the U.S.A.   40

First Scholastic printing, June 1996

SAY CHEESE AND DIE—AGAIN!

1

"Greg Banks!"

A shiver ran down the back of my neck as Mr. Saur called my name. I had been slumping low in my seat in the last row of the classroom. I tried to hide behind Brian Webb, the big gorilla of a kid who sits in front of me.

And I folded my hands and prayed that Mr. Saur wouldn't call on me to give my report next.

"Greg Banks!" he called.

I felt another cold shiver. Then my legs started to shake as I climbed to my feet. Then my throat tightened until I could barely breathe.

I hate giving reports in front of the whole class.

Especially when I haven't had much time to practice. Especially when we're not allowed to have notes. Especially when *half* of our grade in English depends on how we do on this report.

I cleared my throat and made my way up to the front of the classroom. I was halfway there when Donny Greene stuck his big white sneaker into the aisle and tripped me.

I stumbled — but didn't fall. The whole class exploded in laughter, anyway.

Mr. Saur frowned at Donny. "Donny, do you have to trip *every* person who walks by you?" he demanded.

"Yes," Donny replied with a straight face.

And once again, the whole class burst out laughing.

Everyone thinks Donny is a riot. Everyone but Mr. Saur.

Mr. Saur doesn't think *anyone* is funny. That's why we call him Sourball Saur. He probably wouldn't think *that* was funny, either!

Mr. Saur is tall and thin and nearly bald. He never kids around. He never smiles. His mouth is always puckered, as if he's just bitten into a lemon.

Sourball Saur.

He's sort of a legend at Pitts Landing Middle School. Everyone tries not to get him. My best friends — Michael, Bird, and Shari — were lucky. They're in Miss Folsom's class. I was the only one who got stuck with the Sourball.

I stepped up beside his desk and cleared my throat again. I wondered if everyone could see my knees shaking. My face felt burning hot. My hands were cold as ice.

Does *everyone* get this nervous when they stand in front of the class?

Mr. Saur folded his pale, skinny hands on his desk and cracked his knuckles. "Okay, Greg, let's hear your true story," he said.

I cleared my throat for the thousandth time. I took a deep breath. Then I started to tell the story of what happened to my friends and me last summer. . . .

"I was hanging out with my friends. Bird, Michael, and Shari. We had nothing to do, and we were kind of bored. So we dared each other to do something exciting. We dared each other to sneak into the Coffman house."

Mr. Saur raised a hand to interrupt me. He frowned his sour frown. "What's the Coffman house?"

"It's a haunted house!" Donny Greene called out.

"It's where Donny lives!" Brian Webb mumbled, loud enough for everyone to hear. It got a big laugh.

Mr. Saur raised both hands for quiet and gave everyone his lemon expression.

"It's a deserted, old house in my neighborhood," I told him. "We went inside. Down to the basement. And we found an old camera. And that's what my true story is about. Because the camera had evil powers."

Mr. Saur groaned and rolled his eyes. Some kids laughed. But I took another deep breath and continued my story.

"It was an instant camera. The picture popped right out. But it was never the picture we snapped. It always showed something terrible happening.

"I took the old camera home. I snapped a photo of my dad's new station wagon. The photo slid out. In the photo, the station wagon was totaled. Completely wrecked. And then, a few days later, my dad was in a terrible accident. The photo came true."

I glanced around the room to see how my story was going over. A few kids were laughing. Others were staring at me hard. Trying to decide if I was for real.

Brian Webb tried to make me lose it. He stuck his two pointer fingers into his nostrils and twirled them around. He thinks he's funny, but he's just gross.

"I took a snapshot of my friend Bird Arthur," I continued. "At his Little League game. Bird smiled and posed for the camera. But the photo showed him lying unconscious on the ground.

"Then, a few minutes later, a kid hit a line drive. It smacked Bird in the head. And Bird fell unconscious on the ground. Just like in the photo."

I heard some nervous giggles from the back of the room. I glanced up to see puzzled expressions on a lot of faces. Brian still had his fingers in his nose. I turned away. *No way* was I going to laugh at that.

Mr. Saur had his elbows on the desk and his round, bald head buried in his hands. His face was hidden. So I couldn't tell if he liked my report or not.

"Then something even more scary happened," I continued. "I brought the camera to Shari Walker's birthday party. I snapped Shari's picture, standing next to a tree.

"When the photo popped out, it showed the tree — but no Shari. It was like she was invisible or something. And then, a few minutes later, Shari disappeared."

A few kids gasped. Some others laughed. Mr. Saur still had his face buried in his hands.

"A couple of days later, Shari came back," I told them. "But now we were too frightened to keep the camera. So we took it back to the Coffman house. And we met this strange guy, dressed all in black. He was the inventor of the camera. He told us that the camera had a curse on it, and — "

To my surprise, Mr. Saur jumped to his feet. "That will be enough," he snapped.

5

"Excuse me?" I wasn't sure I heard him correctly.

The room went silent.

Mr. Saur shook his head. Then he narrowed his watery brown eyes at me. "Greg," he said, "I have some very bad news for you."

2

The lunch bell rang.

"We'll hear more reports tomorrow," Mr. Saur announced. "Class dismissed."

Chairs scraped the floor as everyone stood up. I watched the other kids gather up their books and backpacks and head for the door. Freedom.

I had an urge to run after them. But Mr. Saur kept his eyes locked on me, holding me in place with those cold eyes.

I waited until the classroom had emptied out. Then I turned to the lemon-faced teacher. "What's the bad news?" I gritted my teeth.

"I'm giving you an *F*," Sourball said.

"Huh?"

"I'm failing you on that report, Greg."

I felt my knees give. I had to grab the chalk tray to keep myself from collapsing in a quivering heap on the floor. "B — but — but — *why?*" I choked out.

He crossed his bony arms over the front of his

7

yellow alligator-shirt. I wished the alligator would reach up and bite him.

"You didn't do the assignment," he said.

"But — but — but — " I still gripped the chalk tray. My legs were shaking too hard to stand up.

"Greg, you were supposed to share a *true* story," Mr. Saur scolded. "Instead, you came in here with that wild tale. It was completely silly. I don't know what you were thinking!"

"But it's *true*!" I wailed. "The camera — "

He waved a hand in my face. "Silly," he repeated. "You came in here with a wild, silly story. Something you probably read in a comic book."

"Mr. Saur — !" I started. I let go of the chalk tray and balled my hands into tight fists. "You have to believe me. The camera is real. I didn't make up the story."

I took a deep breath. Then I struggled to keep my voice low and calm. "You can ask my friends," I told him. "They're in Miss Folsom's class. They'll tell you it really happened."

"I'm sure they will." He smirked at me. "I'm sure your friends will tell me whatever you want them to tell me."

"No. Really — !" I protested.

Mr. Saur shook his head. "You didn't take the assignment seriously, Greg. You treated it like a big joke. So I have to give you an *F*."

I raised my fists and let out a loud groan.

Greg, get control, I warned myself. Get control.

But how could I get control? The grade was so unfair. And it meant so much to me.

It was a matter of life or death!

"Mr. Saur — you *can't* give me an *F*!" I wailed. I felt like dropping to my knees and begging for mercy. "You will ruin my life!"

He stared coldly at me. He didn't say a word.

"If I don't get better grades, I can't visit my cousins this summer," I explained. "You see, my cousins live near Yosemite. In California. And my parents said that if I get a better grade in your English class, I can spend the summer with them."

He didn't move. His cold frown didn't budge. His eyes didn't blink.

"If you give me an *F*, I'll be stuck all summer in Pitts Landing!" I cried.

Finally, Mr. Saur moved. An unpleasant smile spread over his face. His wet brown eyes flashed. "Then you'll have plenty of time to make up more crazy stories," he said.

He turned away from me and started scribbling notes in his black grade book.

"Mr. Saur — please!" I begged. "You've got to believe me. My story is true. I didn't make it up. Please — "

He raised his eyes from the grade book. "Okay. Prove it."

My mouth dropped open. "Huh?"

"Bring in the camera," he said. "Bring it in and

9

prove that it's evil. Prove that your story is true — or else I have to fail you."

I stared at him, studying his face. Was he serious?

He stared back for a moment, daring me with his eyes. Then he shooed me away with both hands. "Go to lunch, Greg. Maybe next time you'll take my assignment seriously."

I gathered up my backpack and slung it over my shoulder. Then I slumped out of the room, thinking hard.

Could I go back to that creepy old house and dig out that camera?

No. No way.

The camera was too dangerous. Too frightening. Too *evil*.

But I needed a good grade. I needed it desperately.

What should I do?

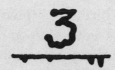

I found my friends at our usual table in the corner of the lunchroom. I dropped my tray down with a sigh, and spilled half my drink.

"Greg — what's your problem?" Bird looked up from his sandwich. He had egg salad all over his chin and cheeks.

"Are you eating that sandwich or wearing it?" Shari asked him.

"Excuse me?" Bird didn't understand.

Michael inflated his brown paper sandwich bag and popped it between his hands. Then he crushed his chocolate milk carton flat. He always gulps his milk down first, then crushes the carton. We're not sure why.

Michael is a little weird.

I dropped into my chair. I didn't start to eat. I didn't even look at my food tray. I just stared at the wall until the tiles became a green blur.

"What's your problem?" Bird repeated. Now he

had egg salad on his forehead, too! I don't know how he does it.

Bird's real name is Doug Arthur. But he looks so much like a bird, everyone calls him Bird. Even his parents.

He has small, birdlike brown eyes, close together over a long, beak-shaped nose. And he has a short tuft of feathery brown hair on top of his head. He's tall and thin and sort of bobs up and down like a flamingo when he walks.

Michael poked a finger through his sandwich. He always makes a hole in the center of his sandwich and eats it inside out. "Bad day, Greg?"

"For sure," I muttered. I sighed again.

Shari wore a pale blue T-shirt over faded jeans. She tossed back her black hair. She was busy pulling the bright red pepperoni off her pizza slice. "Come on, Greg. Spill," she urged without looking up.

I took a deep breath. Then I told them what had happened to me in English class.

Bird dropped his sandwich onto the table. "Sourball didn't believe you?" he cried. He slapped his forehead. When he pulled his hand away, his fingers were smeared with egg salad.

"Well, we could all go tell him it's true," Shari suggested.

I shook my head. "He won't believe you, either," I moaned.

"But we all saw it!" Michael protested. "We all know it's true."

"Yeah. It's four against one," Bird added. He was wiping egg salad off the front of his shirt. "He'll *have* to believe us."

"He won't," I sighed. "You know Sourball. He said I have to bring in the camera and prove to him that it's evil."

"But you *can't!*" Michael and Shari cried together.

I glanced over their shoulders. Brian and Donny were grinning at me from the next table. Brian and Donny are the two biggest guys at Pitts Landing Middle School. We call them Sumo One and Sumo Two — because they're both shaped a little like sumo wrestlers.

Of course, no one has ever called them Sumo One or Sumo Two to their faces. When Donny and Brian get angry, they *sit* on kids and squash them like bugs.

And now, they had followed me from Mr. Saur's class and were grinning at me from the next table. When they saw me watching, they formed little square cameras with their fingers and raised them in front of their eyes.

"Click! Click!" Brian called. "I've got an evil camera here!"

"Say cheese!" Donny shouted. "Say cheese — and die! Ha-ha-ha!"

"Click. Click. Click." They clicked their air cameras.

"Watch the birdie!" Donny cried.

"Watch the birdbrain!" Brian yelled.

They both tossed back their heads and laughed like lunatics, slapping each other high fives.

"Funny, guys," I said, rolling my eyes. "Real funny."

"You two should do stand-up," Michael told them. "You should stand up in the corner!"

No one laughed. No one ever laughs at Michael's jokes. His jokes are never funny. In fact, they are embarrassing.

Michael has short red hair, blue eyes, and a face full of freckles. He isn't exactly fat — but no one would ever call him skinny.

One of these days, he's going to surprise us and make a joke that *isn't* totally lame.

But I was in no mood for jokes, anyway. My summer was about to be ruined. My three friends all had plans to go away. No way I wanted to be left all alone in Pitts Landing with nothing to do for three months!

If I had to bring in that camera to prove to Mr. Saur that I was telling the truth . . . I'd do it!

Shari must have read my thoughts. She reached across the table and grabbed my arm. "Greg — you can't," she said. "That camera is too dangerous."

Bird agreed. "I'm not going back to that weird

house," he said, shaking his head. "Never again."

"Hey — what about your brother?" Michael asked me.

I turned to him, confused. "What about my brother?"

"Isn't he working in a camera store?" Michael demanded.

I nodded. My older brother, Terry, was working at Kramer's Photo Store after school. "Yeah. He's at Kramer's. He works in the developing lab. So what?"

"Maybe Terry could borrow an old camera from the store," Michael suggested. "You can bring it in and tell Mr. Saur it's the evil camera."

"Just one problem," I told Michael. "I have to prove the camera is evil. How do I do that?"

Michael thought about it. And thought.

"It won't work," I sighed. "We have to go get the real camera." I glanced around the table. "Who will go with me?"

No one answered. Bird concentrated on getting the egg salad out from under his fingernails. Shari twisted a lock of black hair around one finger. Michael stared at the floor.

"Don't all volunteer at once," I grumbled.

They still didn't move.

"I just need the camera for one day," I added. "Then we'll return it and never take it out again."

No one replied. Bird raised his beady little eyes to the ceiling and started whistling to himself.

I sneered at them. "Okay, wimps. I'll go by myself."

"Don't do it," Shari warned again. "Not even for a day. Something horrible will happen. I know it will."

If only I had listened to her.

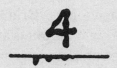

4

The rest of the afternoon, I barely heard a word anyone said. I think I had a spelling quiz. I think we played volleyball in gym. I think someone slammed the ball onto my head.

Did it hurt? Did I have to leave the game for a while?

I really don't remember.

In music class, Miss Jakes caught me staring out the window, a dazed look on my face. She thought it was because of the volleyball accident. She wanted to send me to the nurse.

But I explained that I was okay. I told her I wasn't hurt — I was only daydreaming.

I didn't explain that I was thinking hard. Thinking about that evil camera hidden away in the Coffman house.

Thinking about how I was going to sneak out after dinner. Ride my bike up the hill to the deserted old house. Creep down to the basement —

and pull the camera from its hiding place in the wall.

I'm going to prove the camera is evil, Sourball. I'm going to prove you're wrong and unfair! I thought bitterly.

I'm going to prove it to Brian and Donny and all the other kids who laughed at my story.

I'm going to get an *A* for my report. Not an *F*.

I thought about all that. And I thought about Shari, Michael, and Bird.

I didn't blame my friends for being scared. I was scared, too. I promised myself I'd be really careful.

I'll bring it to school. But I won't take anyone's picture with it, I decided.

Then how would I prove to Mr. Saur that the camera is evil?

I thought hard. I'll take a snapshot of the empty classroom, I decided. Or maybe the lunchroom or the gym when no one is there.

As soon as Mr. Saur changes my grade to an *A*, I'll return the camera, I promised myself. I'll shove it back into its hiding place. And I'll never take it out again.

After school, I searched for Shari. She lives next door, so we usually walk home together. But I didn't see her anywhere.

I crossed the street, kicking a bottle cap I found at the curb. Thinking about my plan. Thinking about the camera.

I had walked about half a block when I heard voices behind me. "Greg! Hey — Greg!"

Two hands grabbed my shoulders and spun me around hard.

Brian Webb!

"Greg — Donny and I went to the Coffman house!" he exclaimed, grinning, holding me in place. "We found the evil camera!"

"Say cheese!" Donny cried.

He pointed the camera and flashed it in my face.

5

I uttered a hoarse cry.

And shut my eyes against the white flash.

Something horrible is going to happen to me now, I realized.

The picture is going to show me in pain. In agony. In terrible trouble. And then it's going to come true!

When I opened my eyes, Brian and Donny were laughing. They slapped each other a high five.

I stared at the camera in Donny's hand.

A yellow cardboard camera. One of those cheap throwaway cameras.

Not the evil camera. Not the old camera from the Coffman house.

"Good joke, guys!" I said sarcastically. I blinked several times, trying to make the yellow dots disappear. "You guys are a riot."

"*You're* the funny one!" Brian shot back. "That was such a funny story you told in class!"

"Yeah. It had us *all* laughing," Donny chimed in.

I stared angrily at them. My heart thumped loudly. Sumo One and Sumo Two. They were so big, they nearly blocked out the sunlight!

I knew they wanted to keep on teasing me. Have some more laughs at my expense. Maybe get into a fight.

But I didn't have time to fight with them.

"Maybe you won't be laughing tomorrow," I murmured. Then I turned, jogged across the street, and headed for home.

At dinner, I stared down at my plate. I was too nervous to eat. My stomach felt as if it were tied in a tight knot.

"Pass the potatoes," my brother, Terry, said with a mouth full of chicken.

"It's not potatoes. It's turnips," Mom corrected him.

Terry shrugged. "Whatever." He scooped a pile onto his plate and began spooning them quickly into his mouth.

"Slow down, Terry," Dad scolded. "You're eating so fast, you don't know what you're eating!"

"Sure, I do," Terry protested. "I'm eating *dinner!*"

Mom and Dad laughed.

Terry looks a lot like me — blond hair, green eyes, kind of a goofy smile. We could almost be twins, except that he's sixteen, four years older than me.

"Why are you in such a hurry?" Mom asked him.

Terry burped. "Excuse me." He licked chicken grease off his fingers. "I have to get back to work. A lot of special orders came in today. So I promised Mr. Kramer I'd put in a few extra hours in the developing lab."

"You're learning a lot about photography — aren't you?" Dad said.

"Yeah. A lot."

Oh, please! I thought. *Please don't talk about photography!*

I knew that soon after dinner, I'd be sneaking out to that creepy old deserted house. I didn't want to think about cameras or photography.

Terry's chair scraped the floor as he jumped to his feet. He tossed his greasy napkin onto the table. "Got to run. See you later." He loped to the door.

"Don't you have any homework tonight?" Mom called after him.

"No," he shouted from the front hall. "They don't give homework in high school!" The front door slammed behind him.

"What a comedian," Dad muttered, shaking his head.

They both suddenly remembered that I was at

the table, too. "Greg — you haven't touched your chicken!" Mom said, staring at my full plate.

"I ate too much junk after school," I lied. "I'm not too hungry."

"Your mom and I are going over to Alana's after dinner," Dad told me. Alana is Mom's sister. "Alana still isn't feeling well. Do you want to come with us?"

"Uh . . . no," I replied, thinking hard. "I've got too much homework. I'm going to be studying all night."

I don't like to lie to Mom and Dad — if I can help it.

Tonight I couldn't help it.

"How are your grades this semester?" Mom asked.

"Yes, how are they?" Dad repeated, leaning closer. "Pete and Alice out in Yosemite called me this afternoon. They asked if you are coming to visit them this summer. I told them we'd know as soon as your next report card arrives."

"Uh . . . I'm doing real well," I told them, staring down at my chicken and turnips.

I'll be doing real well after tomorrow, I thought. My stomach knotted even tighter.

Mom and Dad stood up to clear the table. "Pete and Alice said to be sure to bring a camera," Dad said. "It's such beautiful country out there."

"Maybe Terry can get you a good camera at the store," Mom suggested.

Please stop talking about cameras! I thought, gritting my teeth.

"Maybe he can," I said.

I waited till Mom and Dad drove off for Alana's house. Then I waited ten minutes more. Sometimes they forget something, turn around, and come back home.

I peered out the window. Under the white moonlight, the bare trees were bending and shaking. A breezy night. Still cold even though spring was only a few weeks away.

I pulled a long-sleeved flannel shirt over my T-shirt. Tucked a pocket flashlight into my jeans. And headed out to the garage to get my bike.

The swirling wind felt heavy and wet. I glanced up at the sky, hoping it wasn't getting ready to rain. A pale half-moon floated over the quivering trees.

The front tire on my bike was a little low. But I guessed I could make it up the hill to the Coffman house. I walked the bike out of the garage, then climbed on.

I'd left all the lights on in the house. From the driveway, it looked so bright and warm and safe. For a moment, I was tempted to go back inside and forget about the evil camera.

But my mind was made up. I *desperately* wanted to visit my cousins this summer. No way

I could do that if I got an *F* from Mr. Saur on my report.

I took a deep breath. Clicked on the bike headlight. And pedaled down to the street.

It was lucky that Mom and Dad had to go away, I told myself. At least I didn't have to sneak out of the house.

"That's it, Greg," I said out loud, pedaling harder. "Look on the bright side."

The street seemed darker than usual. Glancing up, I saw that two streetlights were out.

The wind swept toward me. On both sides, the trees appeared to be shivering. I swerved to miss a sheet of old newspaper fluttering across the street.

I shifted gears as the street sloped uphill. I pictured the ramshackle old Coffman house. Hidden behind ancient oak trees at the top of a weed-choked lawn.

I remembered that it stood three stories tall, gray shingle, with a wraparound screened porch, a sloping red roof, and tall chimneys on either end.

Many years ago, it must have been a really fancy house. But no one had lived in it for dozens of years. And the house had crumbled and decayed until it looked like a wreck.

I crossed a street, pedaling smoothly and steadily uphill. Familiar houses rolled past in the darkness. And then a small wooded area.

I felt my throat tighten. And my hands grow cold.

The house — the Coffman house — stood just beyond the woods.

The tree branches swayed, glowing gray — the color of bone — under the cold moonlight.

I squeezed the brake as I rolled past the woods.

Past the sloping lawn. Past the ancient oak trees.

Up to the old house — and gasped in shock.

6

The house was gone.

I jumped off my bike and let it fall to the sidewalk. I uttered a low cry of surprise.

Then I blinked several times. Tried to make the big, old house appear where it belonged behind the oak trees.

But no.

The trees rose up over the lawn, silvery-gray in the moonlight. Now they protected only scattered piles of boards and shingles.

The house had been torn down.

Totaled.

Dazed, I stood at the curb, staring up to where the house should be. Staring hard. Trying to force it to come back.

A minute or two later, I felt a stab of pain — and slapped a mosquito on my forehead. It's too early in the spring for mosquitoes, I thought. I felt wet blood on my forehead.

Rubbing the bite, I turned to the gravel driveway. And saw a stenciled sign near the street: SOLD.

So the Coffman house had been sold.

And the new owner tore it down.

I rubbed the mosquito bite, thinking hard. The house was gone. But what about the basement?

What about the basement workshop? I remembered it so well. I remembered the worktable. And I remembered the hiding place in the wall above it. The small compartment where the camera lay hidden away.

What about the basement?

Before I even realized it, my feet were carrying me up the hill. My sneakers slid over the slick, tall grass. I inhaled the fresh dew. I kept my eyes locked on the trembling silver trees.

I stepped around a pile of rusted nails and bolts. Jumped over a low stack of rotted shingles. Shingles that had been pulled off the house.

Halfway up the lawn, I could see what else was left of the house. Wooden doors stacked in a high pile. Broken glass over the ground. Window frames leaning against a wall of rotting boards. Cracked shingles everywhere. A white sink on its side against a tree. An old washtub resting beside it.

But what about the basement?

I crept closer. My legs suddenly felt heavy. My whole body felt heavy — as if some invisible force were pushing me back, pushing me away.

A deep shadow ran along the ground behind the round, old oaks. At first glance, I thought I was staring at a pool of water. A small lake.

But as I made my way closer, I saw that the deep shadow was a hole. A huge, square pit in the ground.

The basement.

Nothing but a hole now.

I stopped at the edge, my body feeling even heavier. Heavy with disappointment. I stopped and stared down into the deep hole.

The trees shut out most of the moonlight. With a trembling hand, I pulled out my pocket flashlight and clicked it on. I aimed the narrow beam of yellow light into the hole.

Empty down there. The light slid over the dirt. On one side, thick tree roots poked into the open square.

I ran the light over the pit walls. Tangles of roots spread over the smooth, black dirt.

Nothing left. The basement had been completely cleared out. Even the concrete floor had been broken up and carted away.

And where was the camera?

Where?

Had someone found it? Pulled it out and kept it?

Or had it been crushed when the workers smashed the concrete? Crushed and destroyed forever?

I moved the beam of light back and forth along the far wall. I'm not sure what I expected to see.

Did I think I'd find the camera hidden in its square hole in the pit wall? Did I think I would see it in a corner of the muddy floor?

The light swept over dirt and knots of tree roots.

Nothing else.

I clicked off the flashlight and shoved it into my pocket.

I turned away from the hole, side-stepping a pile of broken shingles.

A strong gust of wind made the old trees groan and creak. I barely noticed the eerie sounds.

I'm going to get an *F*, I thought unhappily.

The camera is gone forever, and I'm going to get an *F*.

My summer is ruined. And the other kids in class will never believe me. They will laugh at me and click cameras at me forever.

I let out a long, glum sigh.

Angrily, I kicked a broken board out of my path and started down the lawn to my bike.

I had taken four or five steps when a shrill voice yelled, "Caught you! You're not going anywhere!"

7

The high voice in the night air startled me. Without thinking, I started to run. Then stopped.

I spun around, my heart heaving against my chest.

And saw a boy. About my age. He had picked up a board from the ground and held it high, as if ready to swing it.

He wore a black sweatshirt over faded jeans, holes in both knees. His dark hair was cut very short. He glared at me with dark, tense eyes.

"Dad — I caught him!" he shouted. He had a high, shrill voice that made him sound like a little kid.

"Whoa. What do you mean?" I cried. "Caught me?"

"Don't move," he ordered me, raising the board higher. He took a step closer. Then another. His eyes burned hard into mine.

"I wasn't doing anything!" I told him. "I — I was just looking."

As he stepped up to me, I saw his expression change. The anger faded from his eyes. His mouth slid open.

"You — you're not him!" he stammered.

"Huh? Who?" I cried. "I'm not who?"

"Hey — I'm sorry," he said, shaking his head. "I thought you were someone else."

"Well . . . I'm *not* someone else!" I replied. "I'm me."

"There's a kid who lives down the block," the boy explained, scratching his dark crew cut. "He's been sneaking over here at night and stealing stuff from the yard."

My eyes wandered over the cluttered lawn. "What was he stealing? There isn't much left."

The boy nodded. He tossed away the board he planned to use as a weapon. It clattered against a pile of boards beside me. "He was taking lumber and stuff. I thought you were him."

"Did your family buy the Coffman house?" I asked. Even though it was such a cool, windy night, my forehead was all sweaty. I reached up and mopped the sweat with the back of my hand.

"Yeah. We bought it," he replied. "But Dad said the house was too wrecked to fix up. So he had it torn down. We're going to build a new house."

The wind made the trees creak again. I glanced down to the street and saw the back wheel of my bike spinning.

"People told us the Coffman house was

haunted," the boy said. "So I'm glad Dad tore it down." He kicked at a shingle on the ground. "My name is Jon. What's yours?"

"Greg. I — I live down at the bottom of the hill. A few blocks past the school."

I gazed to where the house had stood. "My friends and I used to sneak into the old house," I told him. "You know. Just for fun. For excitement. I think it *was* haunted. Really."

He narrowed his eyes at me, studying me. "What were you doing here?" he demanded. "Why did you come up here tonight?"

I decided to tell him the truth. "I was looking for something," I said. "A camera."

He scratched his short hair again. "An old camera?"

"Yes!" I cried excitedly. "An old camera. It was hidden down in the basement. Did you see it?"

"Yeah," Jon replied. "The men dug it up when they pulled out the basement."

"Oh, wow!" I cried. I couldn't hide my excitement. "Where is it, Jon? I mean — what did they do with it? Do you know where it is?"

He pointed over my shoulder toward the street. "Probably over there," he said. "I don't think they emptied it yet."

I spun around and saw a big Dumpster on the other side of the driveway. "They threw it in there?" I demanded.

I didn't wait for him to answer. I started running full speed through the tall weeds to the street. I stopped in front of the big steel Dumpster. I could see all kinds of junk piled over the top.

"Is it okay to look for it?" I called back to Jon.

He came walking slowly down to me, hands shoved in his pockets. "Sure. Go ahead. Why do you want a stupid old camera, anyway?"

I didn't answer him. No time for answering questions.

I lifted both hands to the top of the Dumpster. It was pretty high. It took me three tries to pull myself up and in.

A street lamp across the street cast a glow of dim yellow light over the Dumpster. My eyes wandered quickly over the trash. All stuff from the basement, I realized.

I saw rusted old tools from the workshop. Part of an ancient vacuum cleaner. The spin cylinder from a dryer. Old clothes. Torn suitcases.

Is it here? I asked myself. Is the camera in here?

I pulled away a broken suitcase and tossed it aside. I grabbed stacks of old magazines and shoved them out of the way.

I'm going to search every inch of this Dumpster till I find it, I told myself.

I pulled away a torn section of a garden hose. Then I pawed through a pile of old clothes.

Where is it? Where?

I dropped onto my hands and knees and dug

deeper into the garbage. The stale odor of dust and decay floated up to me, swept over me. I held my breath and kept pawing away.

I had to find it. I *had* to.

I didn't stop until I saw the two eyes staring up at me.

Two eyes. Yellow in the pale light.

Staring up at me from the trash. Staring up at me without blinking.

I'm not alone in here! I realized.

And then I opened my mouth in a shrill, terrified scream.

8

The eyes stared up at me without blinking. Yellow and cold.

A chill tightened the back of my neck.

I stared down at them, waiting for them to move. Waiting for something to jump up at me.

"What's wrong? Did you find the camera?" Jon called from the sidewalk.

"No. I — uh — I — "

I reached my hand down toward the glassy yellow eyes. And felt bristly fur.

My heart pounding, I pushed some junk aside.

And without thinking, I picked up the staring creature.

Felt its body, stiff and hard beneath bristly brown and black fur.

A dead raccoon.

Its sour odor reached my nostrils. "Oooooh, yuck!" I let out a groan — and heaved the smelly creature out of the Dumpster.

"Hey, Greg — " Jon called up to me.

"I found a dead raccoon," I told him, holding my nose. "It smelled so bad, I — "

I stopped when I saw the camera.

It had been hidden beneath the raccoon's body. The glow from the street lamp spilled over it. The glass of the camera lens reflected the light like a single, shining eye.

I grabbed it. Pulled it up from the trash.

Then I climbed to my feet. Leaning over the Dumpster, I held it up to Jon. "I found it!" I cried happily. "Here it is. I can't believe I found it!"

Jon wrinkled his face up at me. "Great," he said, without enthusiasm.

I strapped the camera around my neck. Then, holding on to the top of the Dumpster, I lowered myself to the ground.

My shirt and jeans were covered with dust and sticky grease. But I didn't care. I had the camera in my hands.

"What's so great about it?" Jon demanded. He squinted down at it. Rubbed a hand over the top. "Does it work?"

I didn't want to tell him the story of the camera. I knew he wouldn't believe it, anyway. I didn't want to scare him. And mainly, I wanted to get home with it as fast as I could.

"Yeah. It works," I replied, dusting off the back with my hand. "It takes pretty good pictures."

"But why do you want it so much?" Jon asked, studying it as I worked to clean the dust off.

"Oh . . . well. I promised to show it to someone. In school," I told him. "I kind of need it for a project."

Jon scratched his short, dark hair. "Maybe I should show the camera to my dad," he said, motioning behind him. "He might not want you to take it."

"But you threw it in the trash!" I cried. I held the camera tightly in both hands, afraid he was going to try to grab it away.

"But we didn't know it works," Jon replied in his high, shrill voice. "Is it valuable? Maybe it's valuable. An antique or something."

"No way. It's not valuable," I insisted. "Please, Jon. I — "

"We'd better show it to Dad," Jon said. He reached for the camera.

I pulled away.

I grabbed the camera tighter.

Heard a click.

A white flash of light startled us both.

"Oh, noooo!" I let out a cry, realizing I had pushed the shutter.

And snapped a picture of Jon.

9

"Hey — why did you do that?" Jon demanded.

"It — it was an accident," I stammered. I pulled the picture from the slot at the bottom of the camera. "I didn't mean to. Really."

Jon and I both blinked several times, trying to get the flashing lights to fade from our eyes. "It's an instant camera?" Jon demanded. "It looks too old to be an instant camera."

"Yeah. I know," I replied. I held up the photo to watch it develop. Silently, I prayed that the photo wouldn't show anything terrible.

Please, please — let Jon be okay in the snapshot, I pleaded.

With my free hand, I pulled the little flashlight from my pocket. I beamed it down on the photo as it slowly developed.

As I stared at the small, square snapshot, I could see Jon's face come into view. His eyes were closed. His mouth was open, twisted in a strange expression.

Before I could really see what was going on, Jon grabbed the photo away from me. He raised it close to his face and studied it.

"Hey — what's with this camera?" he demanded.

I stepped up behind him to see the snapshot. "Oh, nooooo," I groaned.

The photo came out very clear and bright. It showed Jon howling in pain. His eyes shut. His mouth open in a scream.

His leg was raised. He was holding on to his sneaker with both hands.

He was holding on to his sneaker because a huge nail was sticking up from the top. An enormous carpenter's nail — nearly as big as a pencil — shoved up through the center of Jon's foot!

Jon laughed. He turned to me. "What is this? Some kind of joke camera?"

I swallowed hard. I knew it wasn't a joke.

The horrifying photos always came true.

How could I keep Jon from having a nail jammed in his foot? What could I do?

I decided I had to warn him. I had to tell him the truth about the camera.

"This is cool!" Jon exclaimed, studying the photo. "It really looks like me. I wonder how it works."

"It — it isn't cool," I stammered. "It's really kind of scary, Jon. The camera is evil. It has a curse on it. The photos always come true."

He laughed. "For sure!"

I knew he wouldn't believe me.

"Well, just be careful — okay?" I insisted. "The photo isn't a joke."

He laughed again.

A gust of wind sent the tall weeds swaying. Snakes of black cloud slithered over the moon. Darkness swept over us.

"I need to borrow the camera," I told Jon. "Just for one day."

"It's such a cool camera," he replied. "I don't know. Maybe I should take it home."

"I'll bring it back tomorrow afternoon," I promised. "I just have to take it to school."

He twisted his mouth, thinking hard. "I'd better ask my dad." He pointed to a wall of lumber under the trees. "He's back there with the architect, talking about the new house."

"No. Wait!" I cried.

But Jon took off, running up the hill through the swaying weeds.

I started after him — but stopped when I heard a shrill bleat. And then Jon's horrifying roar of pain soared out over the lawn.

10

My breath caught in my chest. I stumbled forward through the weeds.

And saw Jon holding his sneaker, his face twisted in pain.

Even in the dim moonlight, I could see the huge nail pushing up through his foot.

"Jon!" I shouted. "I'll get your dad!"

I didn't need to find him. Two men — one tall and thin, the other chubby and short — rushed out from behind the lumber pile. I guessed they were the architect and Jon's dad.

"Jon? What's wrong?" the chubby one — Jon's dad — called.

Jon tossed back his head in another scream of pain.

"He's got a nail in his foot!" I shouted, running up to them, pointing frantically.

Both men ran past me. "Oh, good heavens!" Jon's dad moaned.

They grabbed Jon under the arms. The tall man

held Jon's injured foot above the ground. "Into my car," he urged. "I have a towel. We can wrap the foot. He's losing a lot of blood."

"Should we pull out the nail?" Jon's dad asked in a quivering voice.

"No. Too dangerous," the other man replied.

"Don't pull it out! Don't!" Jon pleaded. "It'll hurt too much!"

"We can't even take off the sneaker!" Jon's dad cried.

"The hospital is that way," the architect said, pointing. "Only a few minutes away."

"Owwww. It hurts! It hurrrrts!" Jon wailed.

The two men lifted him off the ground. And half-walking, half-running, they carried him down to a car parked across from the Dumpster.

I watched from the weeds as they gently lowered Jon into the backseat. I saw them struggle with a long white towel. Finally, they had it tightly wrapped around the foot and sneaker.

They closed Jon's car door. Then they quickly slid into the front. A few seconds later, the car roared off into the darkness.

I stood in the middle of the yard, feeling the swaying weeds brush against my jeans legs. I swallowed hard. My mouth suddenly felt as dry as cotton.

"Poor Jon," I murmured out loud.

The camera was as evil as ever. Tonight it had found another victim.

It's all my fault, I thought sadly. It was an accident. I didn't mean to press the shutter. But I pressed it.

The two men hadn't even looked at me. They were so upset about Jon, I don't think they saw me.

I glanced down and realized that I still gripped the camera in my hands. I had a strong urge to heave it to the ground. To stomp on it again and again until I smashed it forever.

My eye caught something fluttering in the tall grass. I bent and picked it up. The snapshot.

I squinted once again at Jon, holding his foot, shrieking in pain.

I tucked the snapshot into the pocket of my flannel shirt. I'll bring it in to Mr. Saur, I decided. I'll bring in the camera and the photo of Jon. I'll tell him exactly what happened to Jon tonight.

I won't have to snap a picture in school.

I have this picture as proof.

So it won't be dangerous. It won't be dangerous at all.

11

The next morning, I gulped down my breakfast. Then I pulled on my backpack, strapped the camera around my neck, and hurried out the door.

I left the house fifteen minutes early. I didn't want to run into Shari, or Michael, or Bird.

I stepped out into a warm day. The air smelled fresh and sweet. I saw a row of tulips poking up through the ground along the side of the house. First flowers of spring.

I loped down the driveway and turned at the sidewalk. The camera felt heavy against my chest. I reached up to adjust the strap — and heard a voice calling me.

"Greg! Hey, Greg — wait up!"

Shari.

I spun the camera behind me and tried to hide it under my arm.

Too late. She had already spotted it.

"I don't believe you!" Shari cried, running up beside me. "You're unreal! You pulled that thing

45

from the Coffman house?" She stared at the camera, shaking her head.

"Well . . . not exactly," I replied. "How come you're so early, Shari?"

"I was watching out the window for you," she confessed. "I wanted to see if you were crazy enough to get that camera."

I frowned at her. "You were *spying* on me? Why?"

"Because I'm not letting you take that evil thing to school." She stepped in front of me, blocking my way.

I snickered. "Who made *you* queen of the world?" I sneered. "It's a free country, you know."

She crossed her arms over the front of her plaid vest. "I'm serious, Greg. You can't take it. I won't let you."

I faked to the left and tried to edge past her on the right.

But she stayed in front of me. I bumped into her — then backed up a step.

"I'm serious," she repeated. "Take the camera home."

"Shari, you're being a real jerk," I muttered. "You can't tell me what to do."

Her expression changed. She uncrossed her arms and tugged her black hair back over her shoulders. "Don't you remember how dangerous that camera is? Don't you remember all the horrible things it did to us?"

46

I gripped the camera in both hands. It suddenly felt very heavy. The metal felt cold against the front of my T-shirt.

"Don't you remember, Greg?" Shari pleaded. "I disappeared because of that camera. Disappeared into thin air! You don't want that to happen to someone else — do you? Think how terrible you'd feel."

I swallowed hard, remembering the night before.

The camera had already injured someone.

"I'm not going to take any pictures," I told her. "Really. I'm just going to show it to Mr. Saur so he'll change my grade."

"Why will seeing an old camera make him change your grade?" Shari demanded.

"Because I have a photo to show him, too," I declared. I pulled the snapshot of Jon out of my pocket and flashed it in front of her face.

"Oooh — gross!" she cried, shoving the photo away with both hands. "That is sick!"

"I know," I agreed, sliding the photo back in my pocket. "The poor kid. I took this picture. Then, a minute later, it really happened to him."

"So I'm right!" Shari declared, her eyes narrowed at the camera in my hands. "You just proved my point — didn't you, Greg! I'm right!"

A car rumbled past, filled with kids on their way to school. A small brown dog stuck its head out the back window and barked at us.

I glanced at my watch. If we stayed here arguing another few minutes, Shari and I would be late for school.

"We've got to go," I told her. I started walking, taking long strides. But she hurried to block my way.

"No, Greg. I can't let you. I can't."

I rolled my eyes. "Shari, give me a break."

"It's too dangerous," she insisted. "I know I'm right. I know it will get you into big trouble."

"Get out of my way, Shari."

"Give me the camera."

"No way!" I cried.

She grabbed for it with both hands. And yanked it off my shoulder.

I grabbed it back.

And the camera flashed in Shari's face.

12

Shari blinked. Her hands shot away from the camera. She let out a startled cry.

"Oh! Sorry!" I cried, backing away. "Sorry! Really! I'm sorry! I didn't mean to — "

The camera felt warm in my hands. I reached for the square photo that slid from the slot.

"Give me that!" Shari demanded. She swiped the snapshot away from me. "What have you done to me?"

"It was an accident!" I shouted. "You know I didn't mean to snap it."

Shari stared down at the square as it started to develop. "What have you done? What have you done?" she repeated. Her voice trembled more each time she said it. I saw that her hand was shaking.

"I told you not to bring out the camera," Shari cried. "I begged you to leave it at home."

"Shari, I'm sorry," I apologized again. "Maybe it won't be so bad. Maybe — "

She swallowed hard. "Maybe I'll disappear again, Greg. Maybe I'll disappear forever."

"No!" I cried. "Don't say that. Please — "

We both stared down at the photo. It developed so slowly. First, the yellow darkened over the white square. I began to see Shari's face.

Was she screaming? Was she howling in pain? I couldn't tell.

The blue tint filled in over the yellow. I could see Shari's face outlined in green.

"You look okay," I told her. "I think you're okay."

"Wait," she said softly. She bit her lower lip. She didn't blink. Her eyes squinted hard as the red and blue tints spread.

The picture darkened. Darkened to black.

I could see Shari's face clearly now. She wasn't smiling. She didn't look happy. But she wasn't screaming, either.

Darker.

"Hey!" Shari cried. "It's a negative."

"Huh?" I didn't understand.

"It's not a photo," Shari replied, holding the square up to me. "It's a negative. The photo didn't come out. It's all reversed."

I stared at it. She was right. Everything was reversed.

"Maybe the camera is broken," I said. I let out a long sigh of relief. "You're okay, Shari. The camera doesn't work."

"Maybe," she said. She handed me the negative. I slid it into my pocket. When I looked up, she had a strange smile on her face.

An evil smile.

"Shari — what's your problem?" I asked.

I should have known. I should have guessed what she planned to do. I should have moved faster.

She grabbed the camera with both hands. Spun it around. Pointed it in my face. And flashed a picture.

"Hey!" I tried to duck away from the lens.

Too late. She caught me.

"Shari — that's not funny!" I cried.

"It won't hurt you," she replied. "The camera is broken — remember?"

I pulled the square from the slot in front of the camera.

My throat suddenly felt dry. Is it broken? I wondered. Will this one be a negative, too?

Or will it show me howling in pain with a nail through my foot — or something even worse?

As I stared at the small square, my imagination ran wild. I pictured my body stretched out like a rubber band. I pictured myself tugging at an arrow through my chest. I pictured myself lying mashed under a huge steamroller.

"Shari — how could you do this to me?" I groaned, watching the colors darken.

Her dark eyes flashed. "You're really scared,"

she said. "Admit it, Greg. You're really scared. Now maybe you get it. Maybe you see why I didn't want you to bring the camera to school."

My hand trembled. I gripped the snapshot with both hands.

The colors darkened.

"It's not a negative," I said.

Shari stepped up behind me and stared down at the photo.

"Oh, noooo!" we both cried at the same time.

Shari started to laugh.

"I don't *believe* this!" I wailed.

13

"This is *horrible!*" I shrieked.

I recognized my face. But I didn't recognize my body.

At first, I thought my head was resting on top of a giant balloon. Then I realized that the giant balloon was *me*.

In the photo, I weighed about four hundred pounds!

No joke. *Four hundred* pounds!

I gaped at the photo, studying my round face and my even rounder body. I had about eight chins. My cheeks were puffed way out. The collar of my T-shirt was hidden under one of my flabby chins. The shirt was stretched tight over my chest and only came down to my belly, which bulged nearly to the ground.

I looked like a really gross mountain of pudding!

"Stop laughing!" I snapped at Shari. "It isn't funny!"

"It's *very* funny," she insisted. She grabbed the

photo, raised it to her face, and started laughing all over again. "You're bigger than Sumo One and Sumo Two!" she exclaimed.

I grabbed the photo back. I stared at the folds of flab hanging down from my cheeks. My face was so huge and puffy, my eyes looked like tiny pig eyes.

And my stomach! My stomach hung down over my fat knees!

"Are you still going to bring the camera to school?" Shari asked. "You won't change your mind?"

"I have to show it to Mr. Saur," I told her. "I'm just going to show him the camera. And the picture of Jon."

"And the picture of you?" she asked, grinning.

"No way." I shoved it into my jeans pocket. "I don't want anyone to see it. Ever."

Shari glanced at her watch. "Come on," she said. "We'd better hurry! We're late."

She started to run down the sidewalk, and I followed her.

All the way to school, I kept picturing my photo. Kept picturing my flabby face, my enormous four-hundred-pound body.

Don't worry about it, I told myself.

The camera is broken. There's nothing to worry about.

Nothing to worry about.

But guess what?

I was worried.

The halls were nearly empty when Shari and I arrived at school. The first bell had already rung.

I hid the camera under a bunch of stuff on the floor of my locker. I didn't have Mr. Saur's English class until just before lunch. And I didn't want to take a chance of Brian or Donny or somebody else grabbing the camera and messing around with it.

I slammed the locker shut and locked it. Then I waved to Bird and Michael, who were hurrying into their classroom.

I wanted to tell them I had the camera. And I wanted to tell them about Jon and the nail in his foot.

But I decided I'd better keep quiet.

Michael and Bird agreed with Shari. They didn't want me to take the camera out again. They were too afraid of it.

And, they were probably right.

I slid into class just as the final bell rang. I ducked low in my seat, trying not to be noticed. I had a long time to wait until Mr. Saur's class.

Today was the first day ever that I couldn't wait for Sourball's class to begin!

Once again, I didn't hear a word my other teachers said. In social studies, Mrs. Wackman was rattling on about bauxite production in South

America. I wanted to raise my hand and ask her what bauxite is! I've always wondered about bauxite. I think it's some kind of South American car. But I'm not sure.

Her voice faded into the background. My mind was busy practicing my speech to Mr. Saur.

"Mr. Saur," I planned to say, "you made a terrible mistake yesterday. But I'm not going to hold it against you. I know you will be fair and change the grade on my report as soon as I show you this."

Whoa.

That's too stiff, I told myself. That doesn't sound like me at all. I'll never be able to get those words out.

I tried a different approach. "Here's the evil camera, Mr. Saur. And here's a picture it took of a boy I met. A minute later, the picture came true. You asked me to bring in proof — and here it is."

That's better, I decided. It's straight to the point.

Will he believe me?

He'll have to, I thought. Photos don't lie.

He'll have to change my grade.

I stared at the wall clock over the chalkboard. Why was it moving so slowly? Why?

Finally, the bell rang. I jumped up, ran out the door, and dove for my locker. Bird called to me from down the hall. But I pretended I didn't hear him.

I pulled the camera from its hiding place and slammed the locker door shut. I tucked it carefully under my arm, protecting it.

I saw Sumo One and Sumo Two across the hall. They were shoving a fifth grader up against a locker. Making him bounce back like a yo-yo. That's their hobby. Making kids bounce.

And guess who is one of their favorite bouncers? That's right. Me.

I spun around and hurried the other way. I didn't feel like bouncing today. And I didn't want Brian and Donny to set their eyes on the camera.

I took the long way around to Mr. Saur's class, jogging the whole way. I held the camera snugly and practiced my speech.

A group of kids were talking in front of the classroom, blocking the door. "Make way!" I cried, pushing through them. I wanted to see Mr. Saur before the bell rang.

I stepped into the room. Blinked against the bright sunlight streaming through the windows.

I turned and ran breathlessly toward Mr. Saur's desk.

But I stopped halfway there.

My heart skipped a beat. And I let out a cry of dismay.

14

"May I help you?" asked the young woman sitting behind Mr. Saur's desk. "Are you okay?"

I stared at her with my mouth hanging open to my knees. I didn't answer her questions. I gripped the camera tightly in both hands, afraid I might drop it.

"Where — where's Mr. Saur?" I finally managed to choke out.

"He's not feeling well," she replied, studying me. "I'm Ms. Rose. I'm substituting today."

"He — he's not here?" I stammered in a high, shrill voice.

She nodded. "I'll be teaching the class today. Is there anything I can help you with?"

I glanced down at the camera. "No," I muttered unhappily. "No. You can't help me."

The room was never this noisy when Mr. Saur sat behind the desk. Kids were shouting and laughing. Someone tossed a balled-up piece of paper at me. It bounced off my shoulder and onto

Ms. Rose's desk. I heard loud laughter from the back of the room.

We always give substitutes a really hard time.

When a teacher doesn't show up, it's always time to celebrate. But I didn't feel like celebrating today. I was so disappointed.

I started to my seat — then turned back to Ms. Rose. "Can I put this in my locker?" I asked, holding up the camera. "It will only take a second. My locker is right out there." I pointed to the hall.

The final bell rang. She held her hands over her ears. The bell was on the ceiling right over her desk.

"Okay," she said when the clanging stopped. "But hurry back. I'm going to be talking about the subjunctive tense today. And you don't want to miss that."

Thrills and chills, huh?

I thanked her and hurried to the door. The long hall stood empty. Everyone was in class.

My sneakers thudded loudly on the hard floor. My mind was racing. Thinking about Mr. Saur. And about the camera. I'll have to leave it in my locker until he gets back, I decided.

I promised Jon I'd keep it only for one day.

But what choice did I have?

I turned the corner — and bumped into Brian and Donny.

"Hey — " Brian grunted.

"Hey — " Donny greeted.

They say "Hey" a lot. I think it's their favorite word.

"You guys are late," I said, trying to hurry past them.

But they blocked my way with their big, wide bodies.

"Sourball isn't here," Donny said, grinning. "He's sick or something. So we've got a substitute."

"Tell me something I don't know," I muttered.

"So we're in no hurry," Brian said. "Why should we hurry for a substitute?"

I tried to slip between them. But they were too quick for me. They squeezed together, and I bounced back off them.

"We're going to switch places." Brian grinned. "I'm going to tell her I'm Donny. And Donny is going to say he's me."

"Good joke," I replied, rolling my eyes. "Very original. Now, can I get by?"

"No way," Donny said, puffing up his big chest and leaning over me menacingly.

"You have to pay a toll if you want to pass," Brian demanded. He stuck out his big paw for money.

"How much is the toll?" I sighed.

"How much have you got?" Brian shot back.

They both guffawed and slapped high fives. They really think they're funny.

"I've got to get to my locker," I insisted.

I tried once again to push past them — and Brian grabbed the camera.

"Hey!" I reached for it with both hands. But Brian raised it high over his head.

"Look — Greg brought his magic camera to school," he told Donny.

"Oooh — I'm scared!" Donny replied sarcastically. He pretended to shiver and shake.

"But the camera is bad!" Brian exclaimed, holding it out of my frantic reach. "It's cursed, Donny! You remember Greg's report."

Donny's ugly grin grew wider. "You mean the report he got an *F* on?"

They both had another good laugh.

"Let's check it out," Brian declared. "Say cheese, Greg."

He lowered the camera to his eye and aimed it at me.

"No — please!" I pleaded. I made another grab for the camera.

But Donny grabbed me and pinned my arms behind my back. "Go ahead. Snap it," he told Brian. "Let's put a curse on Greg. Snap his picture."

15

"No — please!" I begged.

Donny wrapped his huge paws tightly around me and pinned my arms against my back.

"The camera really *is* cursed!" I protested. "You don't know what you're doing! Stop!"

Brian ignored me, of course. He held the camera to his eye — and raised his finger over the shutter button.

"Brian — please!" I wailed.

I saw his finger lower over the button.

Then a loud voice called, "What's going on here, guys?"

Brian cried out and nearly dropped the camera. Donny dropped my arms and stumbled back against the wall.

"Mr. Grund!" I exclaimed.

He's the principal of Pitts Landing Middle School. Mr. Grund is young and has blond wavy hair and a really good tan. He looks more like a

62

surfer than a principal. The girls in our school all have crushes on him.

For once, I was glad to see him.

"Where should you guys be right now?" he asked, glancing up at the clock on the wall.

"Uh . . . we're going to Mr. Saur's class," Donny replied, turning bright red.

"We were just helping Greg with his camera," Brian added. He handed the camera back to me.

"That looks like a valuable old camera," Mr. Grund said to me. "You should be careful with that, Greg."

"I'm trying," I said. "I'm going to lock it in my locker right now."

I pushed past Sumo One and Sumo Two and hurried down the hall. As I reached my locker, I heard Mr. Grund scold them: "Get to class, guys. And don't give your substitute a hard time — okay?"

"Okay," Brian promised.

"No problem," Donny agreed.

I met Shari after school, and we walked home together. "What's up?" I asked.

"I got an A on my math test," she announced.

"Big surprise. You always get As in math," I reminded her.

"So? Maybe I like to brag."

I felt a little strange. Tired. Kind of weak. I

stopped about half a block from my house and tugged off my backpack.

"What's your problem?" Shari demanded. "Why do you keep fiddling with that backpack?"

"I think someone messed with it," I said, loosening the straps. "I had it just right. And now it's too tight."

"Why would anyone mess with your backpack?" Shari demanded. She blew a bubble-gum bubble nearly as big as her head.

I stuck out a finger and popped it.

"Yuck!" she cried out as it stuck all over her face. "Are you impressed? That was my biggest one ever," she declared. "Wish I had a picture of it."

"Don't say picture," I grumbled. "Don't say the words picture or camera." I had already told her at lunch about Mr. Saur not showing.

"Where is the camera?" she asked, pulling gum from her hair.

"Locked up safe in my locker," I said. I turned and saw Michael and Bird running down the sidewalk toward us.

"Did you tell Michael and Bird I have the camera?" I asked Shari.

She shook her head. "No. They'd be too upset. After all the horrible things it did last summer, they never want to see that camera again. And neither do I," she added, glaring at me.

"Hey — what's up?" Bird called. He slapped me on the back so hard, I stumbled off the curb.

Michael laughed. "You guys doing anything?"

"Not much," I replied, straightening my backpack. I still couldn't get it comfortable.

"Get your bikes," Michael urged. "Come on. It's a great day to ride around."

"Sounds good," I agreed. *Anything* to get my mind off Mr. Saur and that stupid camera.

"Let's meet at my house," Shari suggested. "I have to ask my mom first."

Michael and Bird jogged toward their houses. Shari and I crossed the street and headed to our homes, which are side by side.

Mom and Dad were at work. Terry wasn't home from high school yet. I dropped the backpack in the front hall. Pulled a box of juice from the refrigerator and drank it in two long sips from the straw.

I still felt weak. Kind of lifeless. I thought maybe a long bike ride would help get my energy back.

My jeans felt uncomfortable. A little tight. I ran to my room and pulled on my pair of really baggy shorts. Mom and Dad always teased me about these shorts. They say there's room enough for a friend inside them.

But I like them. I think they're cool. And they're really comfortable. I usually don't wear them when I ride my bike. They're so long and baggy, sometimes the cuffs get caught in the chain.

I hurried outside and found Shari, Michael, and Bird waiting for me on their bikes. "Let's go, Greg," Bird urged. "It's starting to get cloudy."

I pulled open the garage door and stepped inside, careful to walk around the black oil stains on the concrete floor. I took my bike from against the wall and walked it out onto the driveway.

Then, I did my high-flying circus riding trick. It's my favorite way of getting on my bike. I lean on the handlebars and heave myself up in the air. Then I come flying down on the seat.

Up I went. Pushed my body into the air.

Swung my legs in the air. Dropped onto the seat.

And both tires popped.

I heard the explosion and then a whoosh of air as the tires flattened against the drive.

"Hey — what's going on?" I cried.

16

"Whoa!" Shari cried.

Michael and Bird burst out laughing.

"Nice tires," Michael said.

"Maybe you should go on a diet!" Bird exclaimed.

"Huh? A diet?" I repeated, swallowing hard. I knew that Bird was only joking. But his words sent a chill down my back.

The snapshot flashed into my mind. The ugly snapshot from the evil camera.

I saw myself all bloated and huge. Like an enormous saggy water balloon.

I felt my face go hot and knew that I was blushing. I saw my friends staring at me. I climbed off my bike. "Guess I jumped too hard," I murmured.

"Maybe you need a tricycle," Michael cracked.

No one laughed. Michael's jokes never make any sense.

I squatted down and examined the tires. I ran my hands along the rubber — and found two big holes. Two blowouts. And they were new tires, too.

I dragged the bike back into the garage. "I'll take Terry's old bike," I told my friends.

I actually like my brother's bike better than mine. It's a twelve-speed, and mine is only ten. He hardly ever rides it now that he's got his driver's license. But he doesn't like me riding it.

"Better not sit on it!" Bird suggested. "Maybe you should just walk it!" He and Michael laughed and slapped each other's hands.

"Ha-ha," I said. "You guys are as funny as a flat tire."

"No. We're as funny as *two* flat tires!" Michael joked.

"Maybe you need a mountain bike," Bird said. "Something sturdy."

"Maybe you need a sturdy punch in the face," I threatened.

"Just don't sit on me!" Michael exclaimed, raising both hands in front of him as if to shield himself from me.

"Are we going to ride or not?" Shari demanded, sighing. She glanced up at the graying sky. "If we don't hurry, we're going to get caught in the rain."

I eased myself carefully onto Terry's bike. Then I followed them down the driveway and into the street.

We rode aimlessly around town. When we

reached the long, narrow park a few blocks from school, we bumped onto the grass and raced as fast as we could.

Bird has the best bike and the longest legs. So he always wins our races.

After about an hour, it started to drizzle, so we turned for home. I was glad. My legs felt heavy. My muscles ached.

As we pedaled through the raindrops, I caught Shari watching me. Studying me.

Despite the sweat rolling down my forehead, I suddenly felt cold all over. Why is she staring at me like that? I wondered.

Why?

The next morning, I woke up with two words on my lips: Mr. Saur.

Today is the day I show him the camera, I told myself, stretching and yawning. And today is the day I get my grade changed.

I stood up, still yawning. Rubbed my eyes. And saw that my pillow had fallen to the floor during the night.

When I bent over to pick it up, I felt a tug on the front of my pajama shirt. The buttons all popped off and scattered over the floor.

"Huh?" I opened my mouth in surprise — and heard a long *rrrrrrip*. It took a few seconds to realize that my pajama bottoms had ripped right up the back.

"Oh, nooooo." I opened my mouth in a long, low moan.

The collar of the pajama shirt dug tightly into my neck. I tried to loosen it — and both sleeves ripped at the shoulder!

My heart pounding, I straightened up and crossed the room to the mirror.

My whole body was trembling as I stepped up to the mirror.

I shut my eyes. I couldn't bear to look.

But I had no choice. I had to see. I had to know.

Slowly, slowly, I opened one eye, then the other. I took a deep breath and gazed at my reflection.

Had the snapshot come true? Did I weigh four hundred pounds?

17

I leaned into the mirror and stared at myself.

No. Not four hundred pounds.

I didn't look too different. A little puffy. My cheeks were a little rounder. My shoulders were broader.

I stepped back to check out the rest of my body — and Mom came walking into the room. "Greg, what are you doing? You're going to be late for school."

I spun away from the mirror. "Mom — I grew last night!" I blurted out. "I — I ripped my pajamas."

She narrowed her eyes at the torn pajama top. "Greg, you didn't grow overnight," she said calmly. "Those pajamas always were a little small on you."

I turned back to the mirror. "They were?"

Maybe Mom was right. Maybe I wasn't growing huge. Maybe it was all in my imagination.

I turned back to her. "How do I look?"

She shrugged. "You look fine."

"I mean, do I look fatter to you?"

She studied me for a moment. "Well, actually . . ." Her voice trailed off.

"Actually what?" I demanded.

"Maybe I'll put *skim* milk on your cereal this morning," she replied.

"Hi, Greg. Putting on a little weight?"

That's how Mr. Saur greeted me when I hurried up to his desk before English class.

His words sent a cold shiver down the back of my neck. But I ignored them. I held up the camera. "Mr. Saur, I want to show you something."

He lowered his eyes to the camera and frowned at it. "You want to take my picture? I already had my photo taken for the yearbook, Greg."

"No," I replied. "This is the camera, Mr. Saur. This is the camera that — "

He raised a hand to tell me to stop talking. "Not right now, Greg," he said, climbing up from his desk chair.

"But, Mr. Saur — " I protested.

He was gazing over my shoulder. I turned and saw Mr. Grund standing in the classroom doorway. Mr. Saur hurried over to talk to him.

They talked until the bell rang. Then Mr. Saur returned to the front of the room to begin class. "I'm sorry I wasn't here yesterday," he announced. "I understand you had a wonderful time learning the subjunctive tense."

I was still standing beside his desk, the camera in my hands. He stepped up to the chalkboard, turned, and saw me.

"Greg, take your seat, please," he said. "We have a lot to do today."

"But, Mr. Saur — " I protested. I raised the camera.

"Take your seat," he insisted.

I had no choice. I sighed and trudged to my chair near the back of the room.

How can I prove that my report was true if he won't even listen to me? I asked myself unhappily.

"Today, we're going to hear more of your reports about true things that happened to you," Mr. Saur told the class. He turned to a girl in the front row. "Marci, I believe it is your turn. What is your report about?"

Marci Ryder stood up. "It's about my cat, Waffles. It's about all the funny things Waffles does around the house."

I groaned. *Bor-ring!* I thought. A few other kids groaned, too.

But Mr. Saur actually smiled. The first time ever!

He practically purred! "I like cats," he told Marci. "I have six of them myself."

Oh, yuck! I thought. Six cats!

I can't sit through a boring report about a boring cat! I told myself.

I shot my hand into the air and waved it frantically. "Mr. Saur? Mr. Saur?"

The teacher's smile faded. "Greg — now what?" he demanded.

"Uh . . . before Marci starts," I said, "can I show you the camera? You know. The one from my report? You said if I brought it in and proved that it's evil, you'd change my grade."

Mr. Saur rubbed his chin and frowned at me. "It's Marci's turn," he replied coldly. "I know we all want to hear about Waffles."

"But, Mr. Saur — you promised!" I cried.

A few kids snickered. My voice was so high, only dogs could hear it.

"Greg, you're not going to change my mind," Mr. Saur insisted.

"But I can prove it!" I pleaded. "I can prove the camera is evil."

A few more kids snickered.

"Greg is evil!" Donny shouted.

It got a big laugh.

"Greg is *baaaaad!*" some other kid shouted.

Another big laugh.

Mr. Saur slammed the chalkboard with his wooden pointer. "Quiet, everyone." He sighed and motioned me forward. "Okay, Greg. One minute. It isn't fair to the others to give you extra time.

74

But I'll give you one minute to show off your camera."

One minute!

I knew that's all I needed.

I felt my shirt pocket to make sure I had the snapshot of Jon inside. I knew that once Sourball saw that photo and heard what happened to Jon that night, he'd believe me.

"Come on, Greg," the teacher urged. "Get up here. One minute."

"Coming," I said. I eagerly tried to stand up.

Tried again.

Again.

We have those chairs with the desk attached to the front.

And I was stuck in the chair. Too fat to get out!

18

What is happening to me? I wondered, feeling panic creep up from my stomach. My big blobby stomach.

I climbed into this chair without any problem. That was less than an hour ago. And now I'm stuck in here. I must have put on a hundred pounds *while I was sitting here*!

"Greg, we're waiting." Mr. Saur rolled his eyes and tapped the chalkboard impatiently with the pointer.

On the fourth try, I finally managed to slide out of the seat. Carrying the camera carefully, I tromped up to the front of the room.

"This is the camera," I told Mr. Saur. "My friends and I found it in a deserted house. Just as I said in my report. The camera has a curse on it, and — "

He took the camera from my hands and examined it. He rolled it over and over. He brought it up close to his face. He raised the viewfinder to his eye.

"No — don't!" I shrieked. "Don't take a picture!"

He lowered the camera. "If I don't take a picture, how will I know if the camera is evil or not?"

I reached into my shirt pocket. "I brought a photo," I told him. "This will prove I'm telling the truth."

My fingers were so fat, I had trouble poking them into the pocket. My hands felt like squishy balls of dough. They were too blobby to make a fist!

I nearly pulled the pocket off as I struggled to take out the snapshot of Jon.

Finally, I pulled it out and shoved it in Mr. Saur's face. "Here. Look!"

He took the snapshot and studied it.

"That boy is named Jon," I told him. "I took his picture two nights ago. He was perfectly okay. But the photo showed him with a nail through his foot. Two minutes later, it came true. Jon got a nail in his foot, and his dad had to rush him to the hospital."

Mr. Saur burst out laughing.

Another first. The first time he'd ever laughed in class!

"It's not funny," I insisted. "Poor Jon was in so much pain. He — "

"I've seen those trick nails," Mr. Saur said, his eyes on the photo.

"Huh?" I didn't understand him.

He handed the photo back to me. "I used to have a fake arrow," he said. "When I slid it on, it looked as if I had an arrow going straight through my head. So I understand how you made it appear that this boy has a nail through his foot."

"No! It's real! It's real!" I cried. "Look how much pain Jon is in! Look at his face!"

"Your friend is a good actor," Mr. Saur replied.

"No!" I shrieked. "He isn't my friend! I don't even know him! You've got to believe me! You've got to!"

Mr. Saur glanced up at the clock. "Your minute is up."

"But you promised — !" I cried.

"Greg, go sit down," he ordered. "You're not going to fool me with an old camera and a joke snapshot."

"You lose, Greg!" Donny shouted.

"You're evil, Greg!" Brian chimed in.

Everyone laughed. I could feel my face growing hot. I knew I must be beet-red.

I felt ready to explode. I was embarrassed and hurt and angry — all at the same time.

"I'd give you an *A* for effort," Mr. Saur said cruelly. "But I'm still giving you an *F* for your report. *F* for fake!"

Everyone laughed again.

I couldn't take it anymore.

I let out a cry of fury — and went running for the door.

At least, I *tried* to run. But I was too heavy to move fast. I could only waddle.

"Greg — where are you going?" I heard Mr. Saur call.

I pretended I didn't hear him and lumbered to the door. I had the camera tucked under one flabby arm. I pulled the door open with the other.

And bounced out into the silent, empty hall.

I could hear Mr. Saur calling me from the classroom. And I could hear the kids laughing and talking excitedly.

I slammed the door shut behind me and kept moving.

I didn't know where I was going. I didn't have a plan. I was so angry. I wanted to scream and cry and punch the walls.

I turned the corner — and saw Shari down the hall.

"Greg!" she called, surprised to see me. "What's going on?"

She was wearing a short black skirt over blue tights. She started to run down the hall toward me.

She took about four steps — and then cried out as her skirt fell down!

19

"I don't believe this!" Shari wailed.

We both stared down at her skirt, which had fallen around her ankles.

She dropped her books and bent to pull it up.

Normally, I would have burst out laughing. But she seemed so upset, I just stood there.

"I — I'm losing weight," she stammered, straightening the skirt around her waist. "I weighed myself this morning. I've lost eight pounds!"

"Oh, wow!" I shook my head. *Why was she losing weight?*

I tried to cheer her up. "Uh . . . eight pounds isn't so much," I said. I knew it was lame. But I couldn't think of anything else.

"Greg — I only weighed ninety to start!" she replied sharply. "Now I'm down to eighty-two. I can't keep my skirt up. All my clothes hang on me!"

"Maybe if you eat a really big lunch . . ." I started.

"You're no help!" she snapped.

"Look at *me*!" I cried, holding my arms out so she could see my big stomach. "I think I put on two hundred pounds overnight! A few minutes ago, I couldn't get out of my chair!"

Her eyes checked me out. She was so upset about being skinny, she hadn't even looked at me.

She squinted hard at me. Then she burst out laughing. "Oh, gross. You look really weird!"

"Thanks a bunch," I sighed.

"What are we going to do?" she demanded. "Why is this happening to us?"

I started to answer — but I heard footsteps approaching from down the hall.

Shari heard them, too. "Let's go," she urged. "Quick — help me pick up my books."

I bent to pick up the books — and the back of my jeans burst open with a loud *rrrrrrip*.

After school, Bird and Michael and some other kids started up a softball game on the diamond behind school. I didn't want to play. I didn't want them to see how huge I was getting.

But they pulled me onto the diamond and forced me to play first base.

Maybe they won't notice anything different, I thought. I crossed my fingers and hoped. Maybe

81

they won't notice that I've filled out a bit — since this morning!

My T-shirt was stretched against my bulging stomach. The shirt was so tight, I could barely move my arms. My ripped jeans fit over my legs like tights.

Maybe they won't notice, I told myself as I tried to trot out to first base. Maybe they won't notice.

"Hey, Greg — " Bird called from the pitcher's mound. "Have you been super-sizing all your meals?"

Everyone whooped and laughed. A few guys rolled around on the grass, giggling like hyenas.

Michael pointed at me. "Hey — it's Sumo Three!" he yelled.

"It's Sumo Three and Four!" someone else called out.

More loud whooping and laughing.

"Give me a break," I muttered angrily.

"Give him a lunch break!" Michael called.

It wasn't funny. But everyone laughed, anyway.

They gathered around me in a wide circle. They shook their heads. "Weird," Bird muttered. "How did you put on two hundred pounds since yesterday?"

I didn't want to talk about it. "Are we going to play ball or what?" I demanded.

I had a strong urge to tell Bird and Michael why

I was ballooning up so fast. I wanted to tell them that I had taken out the evil camera. That Shari had taken my picture. That it showed me weighing at least four poundred pounds.

And now it was coming true.

But I didn't dare tell them. They had warned me not to go back to the Coffman house. And they had begged me not to take out the camera.

If I told them the truth, they'd think I was a total jerk.

So I kept my mouth shut and tried to concentrate on the game.

I did pretty well until I went to bat in the third inning. I hit the ball over the second baseman's head and trotted to first base with a single.

I was totally out of breath by the time I reached the base. But the ball was still rolling around in the outfield. "Keep running!" my teammates shouted. "Greg — go to second!"

So, huffing and puffing, I lifted my heavy legs and made my way to second.

"Slide! Slide!" everyone was shouting.

So I slid into second. Safe!

And then I couldn't get off my back.

I wasn't strong enough to pick up my heavy body. I must look like Humpty-Dumpty! I realized.

I tried rolling. I tried rocking back and forth.

And then I tried calling my friends for help.

I was exhausted by the time I pulled my huge body to my house. Sweat poured off my forehead and rolled down my round cheeks and chins.

My clothes were stretched so tight, I could barely breathe. My jeans were ripped. My shirt pressed against my skin. Even my sneakers pinched my feet!

This is horrible! I've got to get into something comfortable, I decided.

I remembered my huge, baggy shorts. The ones I wore to go bike riding the other day.

I carried my bulky body over to the dresser. Bent over with a groan and pulled out the big shorts.

I tugged them on, eager to get comfortable.

Tugged. Tugged harder. Then gasped in horror.

The huge, baggy shorts were skintight!

20

I put on nearly three hundred pounds that day. By evening, I could barely walk.

"It's an allergic reaction," Mom said.

I stared at her. "Excuse me? What's that?"

"You ate something you're allergic to," she answered. "A person doesn't swell up like a balloon overnight."

Dad squinted at me. He was trying to look calm, but I could see how worried he was. "Do you eat a lot of candy bars after school?" he asked.

Mom shook her head at Dad. "He could eat a thousand candy bars a day! They wouldn't make him *this* huge!" she declared.

"We'd better take him to an allergy doctor," Dad murmured, rubbing his chin.

"We'll take him to Dr. Weiss first," Mom argued. "Dr. Weiss can tell us what kind of doctor to take him to."

They started to argue about what kind of doctor I needed.

I waddled out of the room. It took all my strength just to raise my enormous legs. My chins sagged down over my neck. My big stomach bounced out of the room ahead of me.

I knew that no doctor could help me. I knew I didn't have an allergy. And I knew I didn't become a blimp because of candy bars.

The snapshot from the evil camera made me look as big as a mountain. And the snapshot had come true.

No doctor could slim me down. No diet would work.

Later, I begged Mom and Dad to let me stay home. "Please don't make me go to school tomorrow like this," I pleaded. "The kids will laugh at me. I'll be so embarrassed."

"You can't miss school," Dad insisted. "What if it takes weeks and weeks to get you back to normal?"

"The kids won't laugh at you," Mom added. "Your friends will understand that you're sick."

I begged and whined. I even got down on my fat knees to plead with them.

But would they listen? No.

"Don't be embarrassed," Dad said as I waddled out the door to go to school the next morning.

Don't be embarrassed?

I wore one of his baggy running suits — and it was tight on me!

I felt embarrassed just walking down the street. When cars drove past, I knew the people inside were staring at me. Laughing at the big mound of Jell-O bouncing along the sidewalk.

I didn't want to walk to school. But my parents have a Honda Civic — and I didn't fit in the car!

Kids were staring as I squeezed through the front door of Pitts Landing Middle School. But everyone was kind. No one made jokes. In fact, no one said a word to me.

I think they were afraid to come up to me. Afraid I might fall on them! I really did look like one of the balloons in the Thanksgiving Day parade!

The morning went pretty well. I kept to myself and tried to hide in corners. It wasn't easy to hide. But everyone left me alone.

Until I stepped into Mr. Saur's class.

He was as sour as ever. And he embarrassed me in front of the whole class.

"Greg, I don't think you'll fit into a chair," he said, rolling his wooden pointer between his hands. "Why don't you just stand by the window."

I didn't say anything. I waddled over to the side of the room.

The room fell silent. The other kids didn't laugh. They could see that there was something seriously wrong with me.

But Mr. Saur insisted on giving me a hard time.

"Greg, forget the window," he said. "If you

stand there, I'm afraid you'll block out all the sun-light." Then he smiled.

Again, no one laughed. I think the other kids felt sorry for me. Even Donny and Brian weren't cracking jokes.

"Greg, I want you to go see the nurse," Mr. Saur ordered. "I want her to discuss the four food groups with you. I think you've been eating too much of all four!"

I think that was supposed to be a cruel joke. But no one laughed.

I turned my bulk around and stared at him. Was he serious? Was he really sending me to the nurse?

"Get going," he said, pointing to the door.

I turned and shuffled heavily out of the class-room. I expected Donny to stick out his big foot and try to trip me, the way he always does.

But he stared straight ahead, as silent and still as everyone else in the class.

I was glad. If he tripped me, I knew I'd never be able to get up.

I pulled myself down the hall, thinking angry thoughts about Mr. Saur. Why did he make fun of me in front of everyone? Why was he so cruel?

I couldn't answer my questions. Besides, I felt too angry to think clearly. I'll pay him back some day. That's what I told myself. I'll do something mean to him. I'll embarrass old Sourball in front of everyone.

My angry thoughts followed me to the nurse's

office. But I instantly forgot them when I saw the girl huddled in the chair in the waiting room. I stopped outside the door and gaped at her in shock.

Shari!

It took me a few seconds to recognize her.

Her jeans and T-shirt appeared to be about ten sizes too big! Her arms were as thin as toothpicks. Her face was pale and puckered. Her head had shrunk. It looked like a tiny lemon on her frail, noodlelike body.

"Greg," she whispered weakly. "Is that you in that big body?"

"Shari!" I cried. "How much weight have you lost?"

"I — I don't know," she stammered. "Look at me! I'm shrinking away. I'm so light. It took me hours to walk to school this morning because the wind kept pushing me back!"

"Are you sick?" I cried.

She frowned at me. "I'm not sick, and neither are you," she replied in a tiny, frail voice. "I'm shrinking away, and you're bloating up — and it's because of those photos we took."

I sighed and lifted my huge stomach with both hands so that I could get through the doorway. "What are we going to do, Shari?" I whispered. "It's those photos. You're right. But what are we going to do?"

21

Dad picked me up after school. He had rented a van since I couldn't fit into the car. Dad helped me squeeze through the door. My body took up the entire backseat.

The seat belt wouldn't stretch over my stomach. So we had to forget about it.

"I'm sure Dr. Weiss will have you back to normal in no time," Dad said. He was trying to be cheerful. But I could tell he was really upset and worried.

He drove slowly to Dr. Weiss's office across town. The van couldn't pick up speed because of all the weight it carried — me!

Dr. Weiss is a nice elderly man with bright blue eyes and a long mane of white hair. He talks to all the kids as if they're two years old. He still gives me a lollipop after each visit, even though I'm twelve!

But I didn't think he'd give me a lollipop today.

He tsk-tsked as I climbed on the scale. But he

couldn't get my weight. The scale didn't go high enough!

He had trouble listening to my heartbeat. His stethoscope got stuck in the folds of flab over my chest.

He took all kinds of tests, his expression tense and thoughtful. "We'll send the blood samples to the lab," he told me. "We should have some answers in a few days."

He shook his head and frowned. His blue eyes appeared to fade. "I've never seen anything like it, Greg," he said softly. "I'm completely stumped."

I wasn't stumped. I knew exactly what the problem was.

As soon as I got home, I lumbered to my room and grabbed the phone. It took all my strength to raise my huge, flabby arm and hold the receiver up to the bulging flesh of my face.

I punched in Shari's number. It took three tries. My finger was so fat, it kept hitting two numbers at once.

She answered on the third ring. "Hello?" Her voice floated out so tiny and weak, I could barely hear her.

"I'm coming over," I announced. "And I'm bringing the camera."

"You don't have to shout!" she squeaked. And then she added, "Hurry, Greg. I've lost five more pounds. I'm so light, I'm afraid I'm going to float away."

"I'll be right there," I told her. "We'll figure out a way to save ourselves."

I hung up the phone. Then I carefully dug the camera out from its hiding place in my underwear drawer. I had to bend over to reach into the drawer. I was huffing and puffing, gasping for breath.

If I get any fatter, I'll explode, I thought unhappily.

Carefully gripping the camera, I lowered my bulk down the stairs. "I'm going to Shari's," I called to my parents.

They were in the den, discussing what Dr. Weiss had told Dad.

"It started to rain," Mom called. "Take an umbrella."

"I'm only going next door!" I shouted back.

Besides, an umbrella wouldn't cover all of me.

I peeked outside. It was only drizzling. Not much of a rain at all.

I tucked the camera under the folds of my arm, pulled open the front door, and started to step out. But I stopped when I saw the dark-haired boy walking up the driveway.

Jon!

"Oh, no!" I murmured. I knew why he had come. He wanted his camera back.

But I couldn't give it back. I needed it to save Shari and me.

I watched him walking slowly, his head down because of the rain.

What am I going to do? I asked myself. I can't let him take back his camera. I can't!

I'll duck back inside and hide, I decided.

I tried to back up. Tried to back my heavy bulk into the house.

Too late.

Jon saw me.

22

He waved to me and started jogging toward the house.

I had the camera in my hand. I carefully lowered it to the porch and stepped in front of it. I knew it would be hidden behind my enormous body.

But what was I going to say to Jon? How could I convince him to let me keep the camera for a while longer?

"Hi!" he called.

"Hi," I answered, my voice muffled by the thick folds of flab around my face.

"I'm looking for a boy who lives around here," Jon said, stepping up to the porch. "His name is Greg, and he's blond, and he's about my age. Do you know him? He has a camera of mine."

I stared at him. My mouth dropped open. I could feel my chins drop onto my chest.

"What's his name?" I choked out.

"Greg," Jon repeated. "I don't know his last name. Does he live around here?"

He doesn't recognize me! I realized. I'm so huge, he doesn't know that I'm me!

"Uh . . . yeah. I think I know who you mean," I told him. "There's a kid named Greg who lives over there." I pointed up the street.

"Do you know which house?" Jon asked, turning to where I pointed.

"It's about four blocks that way," I lied. "A big redbrick house. You can't miss it. It's the only brick house on the block."

"Hey, thanks," Jon said. The rain started to come down harder. He turned quickly and jogged down the driveway.

A close call, I thought.

I felt bad about lying to Jon. But I had to lie. I couldn't give him back the camera — ever. It was too dangerous.

I watched him until he disappeared behind some hedges. Then, I reached my flabby hand down, picked up the camera, and bounced across the front yard to Shari's house.

Shari greeted me at her front door. I could see the shock in her eyes when she saw how huge I had become.

I was shocked, too. I cried out in surprise. She was starting to look like a stick figure!

As she led the way to her room, she kept tripping over the cuffs of her jeans, which sagged down over her feet. She had tied a knot in the belt around her tiny waist, an attempt to keep the jeans from falling off.

"If I get any smaller, I'll have to wear doll clothes!" she wailed.

"Did your parents take you to a doctor?" I asked, huffing and puffing as I tried to drag my weight after her.

"Of course," she replied in her tiny, weak voice. "The doctor said to make me drink milk shakes five times a day!"

"I wish *my* doctor said that." I sighed.

I lowered myself carefully onto her bed. I didn't want the bed to collapse under me. But as soon as I sat down, I heard a crunching sound. The sound of wood splintering.

And the bed crashed loudly to the floor.

"Don't worry about it," Shari said softly. "I don't have the strength to climb up to bed, anyway."

"If I get any bigger," I moaned, "I won't be able to get out of the house. I really won't fit through the door."

She folded her hands in front of her. Her fingers were so skinny, they looked like bird claws. With her black hair hanging down from her tiny, round head, and her straight pole of a body, she looked more like a mop than a person!

"What are we going to do?" she wailed.

I patted the camera with a fat, spongy hand. "I brought this," I said. "I thought maybe — "

"What good will that stupid camera do?" Shari cried. "I wish I'd never seen it! Never! Never!"

"I have an idea," I told her. I flicked a fly off one of my chins.

She hugged herself, wrapping her skinny arms around her toothpick body. "What kind of an idea?"

"Let's take new pictures of ourselves," I said. "Maybe the new pictures will show us looking normal. Maybe the new pictures will change us back to the way we were before."

She raised her eyes to mine. I could see her thinking about it, thinking hard. "It's kind of risky — isn't it?" she said finally.

"Do you have a better idea?" I asked.

She thought hard again. Then she lowered her eyes to the camera. "Okay," she agreed. "Let's do it."

23

I struggled to climb to my feet. But my arms and legs were barely strong enough to push up my huge body.

Before I could move, Shari flew across the room. She grabbed the camera from my lap.

"Oh!" she cried out as she nearly dropped it. "It feels so heavy!"

"That's because you're so light," I told her. I tried again to lift my bulk off the bed. And failed again.

"Sit still," Shari ordered. "I'll take your picture first."

"Okay," I agreed. "I hope the new photo shows me skinny." I tried to cross my fingers. But they were too fat to cross!

"Say cheese," Shari said, aiming the camera at me.

"Don't be funny," I snapped. "Just take the picture."

She stared through the viewfinder. Raised her finger over the shutter button.

Then she lowered the camera with a sigh. "It — it's too dangerous," she stammered.

"Shari — take my picture!" I insisted. "Look at us! We couldn't be any worse off — could we?"

She nodded in agreement. Then, with a sigh, she raised the camera to her eye again. It felt so heavy in her skinny arms, she had to hold it up with both hands.

"Here goes," she said softly. "I hope it shows you normal again, Greg."

She snapped the picture. The flash made me blink.

A second later, the white square slid out from the front of the camera. She carried it over to the bed and dropped lightly down beside me.

"Let's see it!" I cried, eagerly grabbing for it.

"Careful!" Shari warned. "If you fall over, you'll crush me!"

I gasped. She was right. Sitting next to me could be extremely dangerous.

"Maybe you'd better stand up," I suggested.

She climbed to her feet, swaying because she wasn't used to being so light. "It's starting to develop," she announced.

She held the snapshot in front of me so we could both watch it. The yellow filled in first. I squinted to see if I could make out my face.

Was it fat in the photo? Or back to normal?

The yellow was too pale. I couldn't see my face at all.

Shari and I both were frozen there, staring at the small square. Not moving a muscle. Not blinking. Watching it darken.

And suddenly, I could see myself.

My huge blobby face. My round, balloon body.

Still enormous. Still enormously fat.

"Noooooooo!" I let out a long cry of horror. "Nooooooo! I want to be changed back!"

Shari was shaking her tiny head sadly, still staring at the darkening photo. "What's that on your face?" she cried. "Yuck!"

I grabbed the snapshot from her and held it close. "Oh, no!" I groaned. "My skin — it's all scaly. I look like an alligator or something!"

Shari grabbed back the photo and studied it. "The scaly stuff is on your arms, too," she said. "It looks like reptile skin or something."

And as she said that, I started to itch.

I glanced down and saw red scales covering my arms. Itchy red patches. I started to scratch. But the scratching made the scales itch even more.

My skin flaked off under my fingernails.

"Oh, yuck!" I moaned. "It itches so bad!"

I scratched my arms. Then I scratched my face. More dry skin peeled off as I scratched. Chunks of skin.

Shari took a step back. She let the new photo

fall to the carpet. "Oh, this is so horrible!" she declared. "You're still huge — and now all your skin is cracking off!"

"Ohh! My back itches so bad!" I wailed. "But I can't reach it."

"I'm not going to scratch it for you!" Shari declared. "It — it's too gross!"

I pulled a chunk of scaly, red skin off the back of my hand. "Do you want me to take a new picture of you?" I asked Shari. "Maybe you'll have better luck."

"No! No way!" she cried. She took another few steps back. "No new picture. It will only make things worse."

Her face twisted in disgust. She swallowed hard. "I'm sorry, Greg," she choked out. "But you look so gross, I think I'm going to be sick."

I tried to scratch the back of my neck. But my arms were too fat. I couldn't reach back there.

I rubbed my forehead. A big chunk of skin dropped off and bounced on the carpet.

"Let's just rip up the photos!" Shari declared.

"Huh?" I gaped at her.

She bent to pick up the scaly new picture of me. "Let's rip them all up," she urged. "I'll bet as soon as we rip them up, our bodies will return to normal."

I stopped my frantic scratching for a moment. "Do you think so? Do you think that's all we have to do?"

"Maybe," Shari replied. "It's worth a try — don't you think?"

I pulled the first two photos from my pocket. The negative of Shari and the first fat photo of me.

"I'll rip these two up," I said. "You tear that one. We'll see what happens."

We both held the photos up. I started to tear mine — then stopped.

"Maybe if we rip them up, we'll *disappear* completely!" I exclaimed.

Shari and I stared at each other. Our hands stayed in the air, ready to tear the snapshots to pieces.

Should we do it?

24

"No!" Shari cried. "Don't do it!"

We both lowered the snapshots.

"You're right," I said. My whole body was shaking. "It's too dangerous."

"If we tear the photos to pieces, we might be torn to pieces, too," Shari said. "Or we might disappear completely and never come back."

I shuddered. "Let's not talk about what *might* happen to us," I moaned. "Look at us. What could be worse?"

"A lot of things," Shari sighed. "We'll think of something to save ourselves, Greg. We just have to think positive."

I stared at her. "What did you say?"

"I said, think positive," she repeated.

Think positive.

"Shari — you just gave me a really good idea!" I cried.

*   *   *

We carried the snapshots to Kramer's, the photo store where my brother works.

It wasn't easy to walk there. I had to stop to catch my breath every few steps. And I had to scratch my scaly, peeling skin. And I had to hold on to Shari to keep the wind from blowing her away.

The walk was only about eight blocks. But it took us more than an hour.

When we finally stepped inside the store, my heart sank to my knees. I didn't see Terry.

"He's in the developing lab," Mr. Kramer told me. He kept staring at Shari and me. I guess we looked pretty weird. A stick figure and an elephant.

I pulled Shari to the lab in the back of the store and knocked on the door. You can't just open the door and walk into the developing lab. If you let in the light, you destroy the film in there.

We waited about five minutes. Then Terry came out. At first, he didn't recognize me. I think he forgot that I had put on four hundred pounds in the past few days.

"Yuck. What happened to your skin, Greg?" he demanded, making a disgusted face. "Have you got a rash or something?"

"I don't know," I replied glumly. "Can you do me a favor, Terry?"

He shrugged. "What's the favor?"

I held up the first two snapshots. The negative

104

of Shari, and the positive of me weighing a ton. "Can you reverse these for us?" I asked.

He squinted at the two squares for a long while. "I don't get you," he said finally.

I sighed. "Can you take the negative and make a positive of it? And can you take the positive and make a negative?"

Shari let out a sharp cry. She realized what my plan was.

Maybe if we reversed the pictures, it would reverse our bodies.

Terry would make a positive of Shari's negative, and she'd grow back to her normal size. Then he'd make a negative of my picture, and I'd shrink the way Shari had.

It seemed to make sense. Was it worth a try? Definitely.

Terry took the two snapshots. He studied them closely. He scratched his head. "I guess I could do it," he said. "But I'm really busy in there. When do you need it?"

"NOW!" Shari and I both cried.

Terry stared at us, then down at the two photos.

I scratched the back of my neck. My arms were so fat, I could barely lift them that high. In a few hours, I knew, I'd be too heavy to walk. Someone would have to wheel me around in a wheelbarrow. No — make that *two* wheelbarrows!

"Please!" I begged.

"I just don't have time," Terry said.

"I'll give you my allowance for the next two months!" I cried.

"Okay. I guess I can find the time. It's a deal," Terry replied. "Wait out here."

He disappeared into the lab. We stood outside the door and waited.

And waited.

And waited.

The longest half hour of my life.

Mr. Kramer kept staring back at us from the front counter. Shari and I tried to ignore him.

I wanted to sit down. Carrying so much weight made my feet hurt. But I was afraid if I took a seat, I'd break it. And I wouldn't be able to get back up.

So Shari and I stood outside the door to the lab. And thought about this new plan.

Would it work? Would reversing the photos reverse *us*?

Finally, the door swung open and Terry stepped out. "Here," he grunted. He handed me the new prints. "Don't forget what you said about your allowance."

"I won't," I promised. "Thanks, Terry."

I gazed at the new prints. Terry had done it right. A positive of Shari, smiling into the camera. A negative of me, weighing four hundred pounds.

"Now, get lost," Terry said, glancing up to the front desk. "Go ahead. Beat it. Before you make me lose my job."

I took Shari's hand and started to pull her to the front of the store.

Poor Shari. She really did feel light as a feather. She looked even paler and skinnier than when we came into the store. Her hand felt like brittle bones.

We stepped out of the store and stopped on the corner. I held the new prints up so we both could see them.

"Is it working?" I asked her. "Do you feel any different?"

"Not yet," she replied softly.

"Neither do I," I moaned.

We stared at the new prints. And waited.

We stood on that corner for at least half an hour. Staring and waiting.

Waiting to feel different. Waiting for our bodies to change.

But nothing happened.

We didn't change at all.

"We're doomed," I murmured sadly. "Doomed."

A chunk of skin peeled off my forehead and dropped to the sidewalk.

25

The next morning, I woke up early, before my alarm. I stretched and yawned. Then I turned and struggled to pull my huge body out of bed.

"Heave-ho!" I cried, straining every muscle.

And I went flying across the room!

"Oww!" I groaned as I hit the wall. I bounced off. Dropped to the floor. Bounced up again.

"What's going on?" I cried out loud.

And scrambled to the mirror. And stared at the reflection of my old face. My old body.

No folds of sagging flesh. No puffed-out cheeks or bulging balloon of a belly.

Me!

I was back!

I squeezed my arms. I rubbed my face. I pulled my hair.

I felt so happy to see myself!

I leaped onto the bed and started jumping up

and down, tossing up my arms, and whooping and cheering at the top of my lungs.

"It worked! It worked!"

Reversing the photo had reversed me!

"Yaaaaay!" I let out a cheer for myself.

Mom and Dad burst into the room, still in their bathrobes. Frightened expressions on their faces. "Greg — what's wrong?"

And then they both froze with bulging eyes and opened mouths.

Mom uttered a squeak of surprise. Dad goggled at me in shocked silence.

"You — you're *you* again!" Mom stammered finally.

"You — you — you — " Dad struggled to say something, but he couldn't. He pointed a finger at me and stuttered.

And then they both rushed over and wrapped me in a tight hug.

"I *knew* it was something you ate," Mom said happily. "Some kind of food poisoning."

"Just an allergic reaction," Dad added, finally able to speak. "I knew you'd be fine in a day or two."

"We knew you'd be fine," Mom declared.

"Yeah. Me, too," I said.

What a lie!

"You were very good during all this trouble, Greg," Mom said, wiping away a tear from her eye with the back of her hand. "You had such a good attitude."

"Yeah. Well . . . I always try to think positive," I told her.

I gobbled down my breakfast and hurried next door to Shari's house. As I ran up to the back door, she stepped out, grinning, waving her arms in the air in triumph.

"It worked! It worked, Greg!" she cried happily.

She came running toward me, her black hair flying behind her head, laughing and cheering. Back to normal.

Back to normal!

Whooping and shouting, the two of us did a wild "Back to Normal" dance in her backyard.

When we stopped to catch our breath, Shari turned to me. "We'd better hurry. We're going to be late for school. I can't wait to show everyone that I'm me again."

"Me, too!" I cried. "But wait right here. I have to get something in my room. I'll be right back."

I turned and started jogging quickly across the grass to my house.

"What are you getting?" Shari called, following me.

"The camera," I shouted back.

She ran faster. Caught up with me. Grabbed my shoulders and pulled me to a stop. "Greg — the camera? Why do you need the camera?"

I narrowed my eyes at her. My expression turned serious. I lowered my voice to a whisper.

"For revenge," I replied.

26

"Greg — don't!" Shari pleaded.

I ignored her. I knew what I wanted to do. I knew what I *had* to do.

I ran into the house. Took the stairs two at a time up to my room. Pulled the camera from its hiding place. And hurried back outside.

Shari was waiting for me on the sidewalk. "Greg — this is crazy," she insisted. "What are you going to do?"

I couldn't stop an evil smile from spreading across my face. "I'm going to take Mr. Saur's picture," I told her.

"NO!" she gasped. "Greg — you *can't!*"

"Watch me," I replied, still grinning.

"But — but — but — " she sputtered.

I started walking toward school, taking long strides. I gripped the camera tightly in both hands.

"Greg — something terrible will happen!" Shari protested.

"I know," I said, unable to stop grinning. "Old Sourball deserves it."

"But, Greg — " She tried to stop me. But I jogged faster, moving away from her.

"He deserves it," I repeated. "He refused to believe a true story. He called me a liar in front of the whole class. And he gave me an *F*. An *F* for a really good report."

"But, Greg — " Shari started.

I didn't let her get a word in. I was too worked up. The closer we came to school, the more excited I got about my revenge plan.

"He's going to ruin my whole summer," I continued. "And he's wrong, wrong, wrong! And then, when I got so huge, Sourball was really cruel. He made jokes about me in front of everyone. He embarrassed me, Shari. He totally embarrassed me."

"Greg — "

"He wanted to hurt my feelings," I declared. I could see our school through the trees in the next block. "He wanted to embarrass me in front of the whole class. He deserves what he's going to get."

"So what are you going to do?" she demanded breathlessly.

I stopped at the corner. "He dared me to prove that the camera is evil. So I'm going to prove it — and get my revenge at the same time."

*   *   *

113

I slipped into class just as the final bell rang. The other kids were already in their seats, just getting quiet.

Mr. Saur had his back turned. He was writing something on the chalkboard.

I stepped up behind him. And waited for him to turn around.

My heart thudded in my chest. My hands were shaking so much, I could barely hold the camera.

I took a deep breath and held it.

This was my big moment. My big chance.

"Mr. Saur — ?" I called softly.

He spun around, as if I had shouted. "Greg!" he cried. "You're looking very slender."

I ignored his words. I raised the camera to my eye.

Time for revenge, I thought.

"I brought the camera," I told him. My voice came out high and shrill. "Remember? The camera from my report? You asked me to prove that it's evil. So here goes!"

I centered his startled face in the viewfinder.

I raised my finger over the shutter button.

He grabbed the camera from my hands.

"Oh, yes! The evil camera!" he declared, staring down at it. "Don't waste it on me. Let's take *everyone's* picture!"

"No!" I cried.

He waved his hand. "Donny and Brian — move

in closer." Then he shoved me in front of him. "Get in the shot, Greg."

"No!" I pleaded. "Mr. Saur — no!"

"Say cheese, everyone!"

The camera flashed.

The white square photo slid out.

Mr. Saur smiled at me. "I think I got everyone in class in the shot," he said. "*Now* what's going to happen?"

I swallowed hard. "Uh . . . we'll see," I replied. "We'll see."

About the Author

R.L. STINE is the most popular author in America. Recent titles for teenagers include *I Saw You That Night!*, *Call Waiting*, *Halloween Night II*, *The Dead Girlfriend*, and *The Baby-sitter IV*, all published by Scholastic. He is also the author of the *Fear Street* series.

Bob lives in New York with his wife, Jane, and teenage son, Matt.

Add *more*

Goosebumps®

to your collection . . .
A chilling preview of
what's next from
R.L. STINE

GHOST CAMP

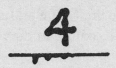

4

"Campfire time!"

Uncle Marv's cry through the screen door shook our cabin.

Alex and I spun to face the door. It had taken us forever to unpack our stuff. To my surprise, the sun had lowered. The sky outside the door was evening gray.

"Everyone is waiting," Uncle Marv announced. A gleeful smile spread over his face. His tiny eyes practically disappeared in the smile. "We all *love* the Welcoming Campfire."

Alex and I followed him outside. I took a deep breath. The air smelled fresh and piney.

"Wow!" Alex cried out.

The campfire was already blazing. Orange and yellow flames leaped up to the gray sky.

We followed Uncle Marv to the round clearing where the fire had been built. And saw the other campers and counselors for the first time.

They sat around the fire, all facing us. Watching us.

"They're all dressed alike!" I exclaimed.

"The camp uniform," Uncle Marv said. "I'll get you and Alex your camp uniforms tonight after the campfire."

As Alex and I neared the circle, the campers and counselors rose to their feet. A deafening "YOHHHHHHHHHH, SPIRITS!" shook the trees. Then a hundred left-handed nose salutes greeted us.

Alex and I returned the greeting.

Chris, the red-haired counselor, appeared beside us. "Welcome, guys," he said. "We're going to roast hot dogs on the fire before the campfire activities begin. So grab a stick and a hot dog, and join in."

The other kids were lining up in front of a long food table. I saw a huge platter of raw hot dogs in the center of the table.

As I hurried to get in line, several kids said hi to me.

"You're in my cabin," a tall boy with curly blond hair said. "It's the best cabin!"

"Cabin number seven rules!" a girl shouted.

"This is an awesome camp," the kid in front of me turned to say. "You're going to have a great time, Harry."

They seemed to be really nice kids. Up ahead,

a boy and a girl were having a playful shoving match, trying to knock each other out of line. Other kids began cheering them on.

The fire crackled behind me. The orange light from its flames danced over everyone's white shorts and shirts.

I felt a little weird, not being dressed in white. I was wearing an olive-green T-shirt and faded denim cutoffs. I wondered if Alex felt weird, too.

I turned and searched for him in the line. He was behind me, talking excitedly to a short blond boy. I felt glad that Alex had found a friend so fast.

Two counselors handed out the hot dogs. I suddenly realized I was *starving*. Mom had packed sandwiches for Alex and me to eat on the bus. But we were too excited and nervous to eat them.

I took the hot dog and turned to the crackling fire. Several kids were already huddled around the fire, poking their hot dogs on long sticks into the flames.

Where do I get a stick? I asked myself, glancing around.

"The sticks are over there," a girl's voice called from behind me — as if she had read my mind.

I turned and saw a girl about my age, dressed in white, of course. She was very pretty, with dark eyes and shiny black hair, pulled back in a ponytail that fell down her back. Her skin was so pale, her dark eyes appeared to glow.

She smiled at me. "New kids never know where to find the sticks," she said. She led the way to a pile of sticks leaning against a tall pine tree. She picked up two of them and handed one to me.

"Your name is Harry, right?" she asked. She had a deep, husky voice for a girl. Like she was whispering all the time.

"Yeah. Harry Altman," I told her.

I suddenly felt very shy. I don't know why. I turned away from her and shoved the hot dog onto the end of the stick.

"My name is Lucy," she said, making her way to the circle of kids around the fire.

I followed her. The kids' faces were all flickering orange and yellow in the firelight. The aroma of roasting hot dogs made me feel even hungrier.

Four girls were huddled together, laughing about something. I saw a boy eating his roasted hot dog right off the stick.

"Gross," Lucy said, making a disgusted face. "Let's go over here."

She led me to the other side of the campfire. Something popped in the fire. It sounded like a firecracker exploding. We both jumped. Lucy laughed.

We sat down on the grass, raised the long sticks, and poked our hot dogs into the flames. The fire was roaring now. I could feel its heat on my face.

"I like mine really black," Lucy said. She turned her stick and pushed it deeper into the flames. "I just love that burnt taste. How about you?"

I opened my mouth to answer her — but my hot dog fell off the stick. "Oh no!" I cried. I watched it fall into the sizzling, red-hot blanket of flames.

I turned to Lucy. And to my surprise — to my *horror* — she leaned forward.

Stuck her hand deep into the fire.

Grabbed my hot dog from the burning embers and lifted it out.

5

I jumped to my feet. "Your hand!" I shrieked.

Yellow flames leaped over her hand and up her arm.

She handed me the hot dog. "Here," she said calmly.

"But your hand!" I cried again, gaping in horror.

The flames slowly burned low on her skin. She glanced down at her hand. Confused. As if she didn't know why I was in such a panic.

"Oh! Hey — !" she finally cried. Her dark eyes grew wide. "Ow! That was hot!" she exclaimed.

She shook her hand hard. Shook it until the flames went out.

Then she laughed. "At least I rescued your poor hot dog. Hope you like yours burned!"

"But — but — but — " I sputtered. I stared at her hand and arm. The flames had spread all over her skin. But I couldn't see any burns. Not a mark.

"The buns are over there," she said. "You want some potato chips?"

I kept staring at her hand. "Should we find the nurse?" I asked.

She rubbed her arm and wrist. "No. I'm fine. Really." She wiggled her fingers. "See?"

"But the fire — "

"Come on, Harry." She pulled me back to the food table. "It's almost time for the campfire activities to start."

I ran into Alex at the food table. He was still hanging out with the short blond boy.

"I made a friend already," Alex told me. He had a mouthful of potato chips. "His name is Elvis. Do you believe it? Elvis McGraw. He's in our cabin."

"Cool," I muttered. I was still thinking about the flames rolling up and down Lucy's arm.

"This is a great camp," Alex declared. "Elvis and I are going to try out for the talent show *and* the musical."

"Cool," I repeated.

I grabbed a hot dog bun and tossed some potato chips on my plate. Then I searched for Lucy. I saw her talking to a group of girls by the fire.

"Yohhhhhhhh, Spirits!" a deep voice bellowed. No way anyone could mistake that cry. It had to be Uncle Marv.

"Places around the council fire, everyone!" he ordered. "Hurry — places, everyone!"

Holding plates and cans of soda, everyone scurried to form a circle around the fire. The girls all sat together and the boys all sat together. I guessed each cabin had its own place.

Uncle Marv led Alex and me to a spot in the middle.

"Yohhhhhhhh, Spirits!" he cried again, so loud the fire trembled!

Everyone repeated the cry and gave the salute.

"We'll begin by singing our camp song," Uncle Marv announced.

Everyone stood up. Uncle Marv started singing, and everyone joined in.

I tried to sing along. But of course I didn't know the words. Or the tune.

The song kept repeating the line, "We have the spirit — and the spirit has us."

I didn't really understand it. But I thought it was pretty cool.

It was a long song. It had a lot of verses. And it always came back to: "We have the spirit — and the spirit has us."

Alex was singing at the top of his lungs. What a show-off! He didn't know the words, either. But he was faking it. And singing as loud as he could.

Alex is so crazy about his beautiful singing voice and his perfect pitch. He has to show it off whenever he can.

I gazed past my brother. His new friend, Elvis,

had his head tossed back and his mouth wide open. He was singing at the top of his lungs, too.

I think Alex and Elvis were having some kind of contest. Seeing who could sing the leaves off the trees!

The only problem? Elvis was a *terrible* singer!

He had a high, whiny voice. And his notes were all coming out sour.

As my dad would say, "He couldn't carry a tune in a wheelbarrow!"

I wanted to cover my ears. But I was trying to sing along, too.

It wasn't easy with the two of them beside me. Alex sang so loud, I could see the veins in his neck pulsing. Elvis tried to drown him out with his sour, off-key wails.

My face felt hot.

At first, I thought it was the heat from the blazing campfire. But then I realized I was blushing.

I felt so embarrassed by Alex. Showing off like that on his first night at camp.

Uncle Marv wasn't watching. He had wandered over to the girls' side of the fire, singing as he walked.

I slipped back, away from the fire.

I felt too embarrassed to stay there. I'll sneak back into place as soon as the song is over, I decided.

I just couldn't sit there and watch my brother act like a total jerk.

The camp song continued. "We have the spirit — and the spirit has us," everyone sang.

Doesn't the song ever end? I wondered. I backed away, into the trees. It felt a lot cooler as soon as I moved away from the fire.

Even back here, I could hear Alex singing his heart out.

I've got to talk to him, I told myself. I've got to tell him it isn't cool to show off like that.

"Ohh!" I let out a sharp cry as I felt a tap on my shoulder.

Someone grabbed me from behind.

"Hey — !" I spun around to face the trees. Squinted into the darkness.

"Lucy! What are *you* doing back here?" I gasped.

"Help me, Harry," she pleaded in a whisper. "You've got to help me."

A chill ran down my back. "Lucy — what's wrong?" I whispered.

She opened her mouth to reply. But Uncle Marv's booming voice interrupted.

"Hey, you two!" the camp director shouted. "Harry! Lucy! No sneaking off into the woods!"

The campers all burst out laughing. I could feel my face turning hot again. I'm one of those kids who blushes very easily. I hate it — but what can I do?

Everyone stared at Lucy and me as we made our way back to the fire. Alex and Elvis were slapping high fives and laughing at us.

Uncle Marv kept his eyes on me as I trudged back. "I'm glad you make friends so easily, Harry," he boomed. And all the campers started laughing at Lucy and me again.

I felt so embarrassed, I wanted to shrivel up and disappear.

But I was also worried about Lucy.

Had she followed me to the woods? Why?

Why did she ask me to help her?

I sat down between Lucy and Elvis. "Lucy — what's wrong?" I whispered.

She just shook her head. She didn't look at me.

"Now I'm going to tell the two ghost stories," Uncle Marv announced.

To my surprise, some kids gasped. Everyone suddenly became silent.

The crackling of the fire seemed to get louder. Behind the pop and crack of the darting flames, I heard the steady whisper of wind through the pine trees.

I felt a chill on the back of my neck.

Just a cool breeze, I told myself.

Why did everyone suddenly look so solemn? So frightened?

"The two ghost stories of Camp Spirit Moon have been told from generation to generation," Uncle Marv began. "They are tales that will be told for all time, for as long as dark legends are told."

Across the fire, I saw a couple of kids shiver.

Everyone stared into the fire. Their faces were set. Grim. Frightened.

It's only a ghost story, I told myself. Why is everyone acting so weird?

The campers must have heard these ghost stories already this summer. So why do they look so terrified?

I snickered.

How can *anyone* be afraid of a silly camp ghost story?

I turned to Lucy. "What's up with these kids?" I asked.

She narrowed her dark eyes at me. "Aren't you afraid of ghosts?" she whispered.

"Ghosts?" I snickered again. "Alex and I don't believe in ghosts," I told her. "And ghost stories never scare us. Never!"

She leaned close to me. And whispered in my ear: "You might change your mind — after tonight."

The joke's on them!

Goosebumps®

Harry and his brother, Alex, are
dying to fit in at Camp Spirit Moon.
But this camp is so weird.
There's a goofy left-handed camp salute.
Strange blue puddles on the cabin floor.
And all of the old campers love to play jokes,
especially on new campers.
But when the jokes start to get out of hand,
Harry and Alex decide to get out of camp—
Before it's too late!

Ghost Camp
Goosebumps #45
by R.L. Stine

Appearing soon at a bookstore near you.

GET Goosebumps®
by R.L. Stine

❑ BAB56879-5	**#42 Egg Monsters from Mars**	$3.99
❑ BAB56880-9	**#43 The Beast from the East**	$3.99
❑ BAB56881-7	**#44 Say Cheese and Die–Again!**	$3.99
❑ BAB56644-X	**Goosebumps 1996 Calendar**	$9.95
❑ BAB62836-4	**Tales to Give You Goosebumps** **Book & Light Set Special Edition #1**	$11.95
❑ BAB26603-9	**More Tales to Give You Goosebumps** **Book & Light Set Special Edition #2**	$11.95
❑ BAB74150-4	**Even More Tales to Give You Goosebumps** **Book and Boxer Shorts Pack Special Edition #3**	$14.99
❑ BAB55323-2	**Give Yourself Goosebumps Book #1:** **Escape from the Carnival of Horrors**	$3.99
❑ BAB56645-8	**Give Yourself Goosebumps Book #2:** **Tick Tock, You're Dead**	$3.99
❑ BAB56646-6	**Give Yourself Goosebumps Book #3:** **Trapped in Bat Wing Hall**	$3.99
❑ BAB67318-1	**Give Yourself Goosebumps Book #4:** **The Deadly Experiments of Dr. Eeek**	$3.99
❑ BAB67319-X	**Give Yourself Goosebumps Book #5:** **Night in Werewolf Woods**	$3.99
❑ BAB67320-3	**Give Yourself Goosebumps #6:** **Beware of the Purple Peanut Butter**	$3.99
❑ BAB53770-9	**The Goosebumps Monster Blood Pack**	$11.95
❑ BAB50995-0	**The Goosebumps Monster Edition #1**	$12.95
❑ BAB60265-9	**Goosebumps Official Collector's Caps** **Collecting Kit**	$5.99
❑ BAB73906-9	**Goosebumps Postcard Book**	$7.95

Scare me, thrill me, mail me GOOSEBUMPS now!

Available wherever you buy books, or use this order form. Scholastic Inc., P.O. Box 7502,
2931 East McCarty Street, Jefferson City, MO 65102

Please send me the books I have checked above. I am enclosing $_____ (please add $2.00 to cover shipping and handling). Send check or money order — no cash or C.O.D.s please.

Name _____ Age _____

Address _____

City _____ State/Zip _____

Please allow four to six weeks for delivery. Offer good in the U.S. only. Sorry, mail orders are not available to residents of Canada. Prices subject to change.

Magic at the Mall

While hanging out at the mall, you find a magic shop owned by a weird old man called "The Magician." When you take his book of magic spells...the trouble begins. Suddenly, you're back in the evil Magician's workshop. Try to hide and you'll end up battling a vicious lion. Choose to become part of a magic act and you'll be stuffed inside a box about to be pierced with razor-sharp swords. What will you do? Choose from more than 20 spooky endings!

#7 Under the Magician's Spell

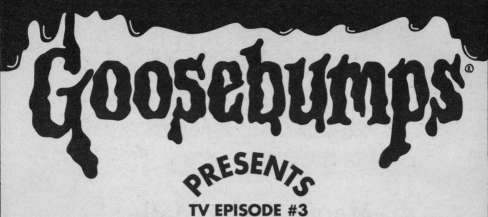